THE PERFECT SHOT

D1584901

WALTHAM FOREST LIBRARIES

904 000 00699264

DICK, KERR GIRLS

THE PERFECT SHOT

EVE AINSWORTH

With thanks to Gail Newsham, official archivist
of the Dick, Kerr Ladies football team; Mike Hill of the
Lancashire Post and Preston historian Keith Johnson.

WALTHAM FOREST LIBRARIES	
904 000 00699264	
Askews & Holts	15-Jun-2021
JF STO	

978-19129795-3-0

1 3 5 7 9 10 8 6 4 2

The right of Eve Ainsworth to be identified as
the author and illustrator of this work respectively has been asserted
in accordance with the Copyright, Designs and Patents Act 1988.

All rights reserved. No part of this publication may be reproduced,
stored in a retrieval system, or transmitted in any form or by any means,
electronic, mechanical, photocopying, recording or otherwise,
without the prior permission of the publishers.

Set in 11.5/18pt Kingfisher by Amy Cooper

A CIP catalogue record for this book is available from the British Library.

Printed and bound in Great Britain by Clays Ltd, Elcograf S.p.A.

This book is dedicated to my Grandad Ernest, and Great-Grandads George Mitchell and William Ainsworth. I never knew you, but your experiences and bravery in World War One live on in our memories and gratitude. So many sacrificed so much for our freedoms.

Lest we forget.

November 1918

I hate it here.

The mud and cold cling to me like limpets on the beach. No matter what I do, I can't keep myself warm. I stamp my feet, but they are blocks of ice attached to my stiff, bruised legs. My toes are completely numb. I stretch out my fingers, but they no longer look like mine. They are brown with dirt, and dry as dust. They remind me of those of an old man. It's as if they no longer belong to me.

I am changing day by day. My body is struggling. My brain is shutting down. My heart is aching.

All around me is the constant sound of gunfire; it never ends.

I stare up at the inky sky. My eyes squint, desperate to see the stars; desperate to see anything that reminds me of home. Of hope. But there is nothing. Only thick, sludgy darkness.

I'm beginning to forget.

I'm beginning to forget what it was like for me before.

And I think that's what scares me that most.

I don't want this to be my last memory.

I just want to go home.

I woke up, shivering and clutching my blankets.

This was my life now.

The sunrise was such a relief. I got out of bed quickly, keen to escape the horrors of my night before. I longed to be outside, in the fresh air, away from the confines of the house and the nasty images in my head.

I carefully made my way down the street, moving with the heavy mark of a war cripple. I didn't really like too many people to see me, in case they made a comment. Although most people were kind, of course, I hated hearing the same things being said.

Oh lad, you're so brave. A hero.

Or...

You've done a good thing for our country.

Or...

We are so proud of you, boy, so very proud.

Each time, I'd mutter my thanks, welcome their prayers and wish them well. What else could I do? Admit to them that the last thing I felt like was a hero?

I had just been a young boy, like so many others, bored of life, who had somehow been swept up in the idea that was sold to us – that we could make our country great again.

Ha! That was some joke!

And now, here I was, left with a gammy leg, a poorly head that thumped most days and a frazzled temper that snapped at a moment's notice.

Most days I walked with my head tipped away from others. I walked to try and strengthen my useless leg, but I also walked to get away from the probing questions of my sisters and Mam. Oh, I knew they only cared about me, but their constant fussing was wearing. I tried to keep my smile turned on. I tried desperately to be the Freddie that they remembered from before, but it was so hard. They didn't know how much I had changed. The scars I wore went far beneath the physical wounds that they had helped to dress. I had changed in ways that they would never know.

It was the sad eyes of my father that upset me the most. I didn't know what was worse – the constant pain in my limb, or the anguish that I saw in his eyes every day. I knew exactly what he was thinking – that I was nothing better than a cripple now.

So, I walked to get away. Most of the time I was lost in a fog of my own thoughts – I never noticed much of what was going on around me. But this morning felt quite different.

This morning I knew something had changed.

I couldn't quite put a finger on what it was about the day. The sky was bright and blue, there was a chill in the air – of course there was, it was November, after all – but there was also a sense of calm. As I walked, I heard people singing in their houses. The baker's boy passed by, whistling out loud. A delivery driver called out heartily across the street.

'Good morning! Good morning!'

His booming voice broke through the chilly air and made me smile.

It wasn't as if people weren't usually friendly round our way, because I would argue to any that Preston was one the friendliest towns in the world. But today, voices seemed brighter, faces were lit up and smiles were wider. There was a sense of pure joy everywhere. I swear, it was so overwhelming I could've bottled it. A trickle of excitement bubbled through me.

'Could it be?' I whispered. 'Has it actually happened?'

There had been rumours, of course, talk that had been circulating for days. Even Dad, who was never one for gossip, mentioned that the lads down the dock were debating things they had heard, whispers about what could happen next. But I don't think he dared to believe it could be true. Nobody did.

'It could be soon,' he'd said cautiously last night, his hand stroking his face. 'It could be. We'll have to wait and see.'

My sister Hettie had been far more positive. The talk at the Dick, Kerr factory, where she worked, had been more excitable, and she was hearing all sorts of gossip. The girls that worked in the factory were now daring to believe that the end was in sight.

'I think it could be any day now,' Hettie had told me. 'I really do.'

And yet, I hadn't dared to hope. What if the rumours were wrong? What if it all started up again? How could anyone be sure?

However, there was little doubt that something was happening today. I could almost feel the excitement like a river, building up strength and rushing towards me, wanting to sweep me up with it. I realised that I couldn't walk any further. I needed to be at home, with my family. I wanted to know what they had heard.

I turned around and headed back. I walked quickly, ignoring the pain grinding in my leg. I heard whoops of joy behind me and the sound of people rushing from their homes, doors slamming, people laughing.

Someone honked a horn loudly, making me jump, and I found myself chuckling at my reaction. This was all so strange, so different to the months before. I had forgotten what joy felt like.

The door of our house was already open when I arrived; my youngest sister Martha was outside in the street with some lads, already kicking a ball around. She didn't even notice me approaching. Hettie stood in the doorway with one of her friends from the factory, Flo Redford, and they were huddled together as if they were sharing some kind of secret. Hettie beamed when she saw me, her entire face lit up like a candle. She pulled away from Flo and ran towards me. Her dress flapped in the breeze and her curls lifted around her face.

'Oh, Freddie!' she gushed. 'You came back early. I'm so glad. Did you hear?'

'Is it true?' I gulped, hardly daring to ask. 'Has it happened? Has it really happened?'

As if on cue, we heard the sudden toll of the church bells. Eleven strikes. The sound had never been so rich, so true. It seemed to rip through the air with defiance.

Eleven strikes on the eleventh month.

'Yes, yes! The Armistice was signed at five o'clock

this morning.' Hettie grabbed my hands and squeezed them in hers. 'It's true. It really is. It's over, finally. This bloomin' war is over.'

Later, in the market square, the church bells continued to toll. We watched in silence and wonder as the trumpeters of the Royal Field Artillery stood on the town hall balcony and sounded the Last Post. A rush of sadness overtook me as the mournful tune echoed across the silent square. Hettie gripped my hand and I felt the heat rising from her body and rushing into mine. I wondered why I still couldn't feel as excited as she did. I was relieved, I suppose, but I also felt tired of it all.

And sad. So very sad.

Johnnie should've been here to see this. But he can't be. Because of me.

'This is it, Freddie,' Hettie said, her eyes wide and focused on the trumpeters. I could see tears glistening like tiny gems on her cheeks. 'It's over. We can get on now.'

Mam, Martha and Dad were also with us. Martha was playing with some of the younger children in the square. Dad was silent in his best suit, his face sullen and grey, and Mam was wearing her Sunday-best dress and smart hat. She looked quite a picture. Both of them stood quite stiffly at the side of the crowd, watching as the merriment began.

'The war should never have happened,' Dad grumbled, his eyes lingering a bit too long on me, on my bad leg. I saw a shadow cross his face. 'But it's good that's all over now. Hopefully this country can get itself back on its feet again, focus on what's needed.'

Mam nodded. 'They need to get our boys home safely. That's the most important thing.'

Those who are left, I thought numbly.

Flags seemed to appear from nowhere and were being waved with gay abandon. The square itself was filling up fast with a cheering, squalling crowd. I don't think I had ever seen such joyous and happy people. The noise they made was like no other, as they cheered and roared in a huge cacophony of sound. It was hard not to be swept up in the excitement and yet, I felt as if I were an observer, watching from outside.

'Shall we stay, Fred?' Hettie said. 'There's going to be bands and all sorts. It sounds grand. Perhaps there'll be dancing?'

I agreed, even though my leg was throbbing a treat and I certainly wouldn't be able to dance with her. But I didn't want to leave Hettie on her own, knowing fine well that Mam and Dad would leave soon with Martha.

Mam cast me a doubtful look. 'Are you sure you want to stay, lad? Shouldn't you be resting that leg of yours?'

Dad tugged on her arm. 'Leave the poor boy alone. If he says he wants to stay, he wants to stay. He's old enough to know what he wants.'

I nodded briskly to both of them. 'Aye, I'll be fine,' I said brightly. 'I want to stay. I want to be here to celebrate.'

By mid-afternoon, the band were playing with gusto. People were dancing and singing along. I found myself sitting beside Hettie, awkwardly but at least a little comfortably, on the town hall steps.

Hettie waved at some of the women from the Dick, Kerr factory, many of whom had played football with her for the factory's women's team. I had watched the girls a few times now and I had to admit, they weren't half bad. I knew it made Hettie sad that she could no longer play, after she got a nasty injury to her knee, but she was still very much involved in the team, helping to organise the games and fundraising with the manager – her boss, Mr Frankland. She was also very keen to get me involved – although part of me wondered if she just felt sorry for me and wanted to help keep me occupied in some way. I wasn't really sure how I felt about that.

Flo Redford and Alice Kell, two of Hettie's closest friends in the team, joined us on the steps. They were both very cheerful, friendly girls and I felt myself relax in their company. It was as if I'd known them for a very long time.

'The plan is, Freddie will take team photos for us with his new camera,' Hettie was saying excitedly. 'We need some for this season.'

'That would be nice,' Flo agreed, nodding. 'I just hope you can get a good one of me!'

I smiled. 'I'll do my best.' I carefully shifted so that my leg didn't cramp up in its current position.

'Are you all right?' Hettie asked, instantly fretting.

'I'm fine. Stop mithering,' I said, flapping her away. 'So, tell me – what will happen with the girls' team now?'

'What do you mean?' Alice asked, quite sharply.

'I mean – now that the war is over. Our lads will be returning. Will you still be needed, do you think?'

The Dick, Kerr girls' team was originally set up to raise funds for injured soldiers and they had done exceptionally well, raising far more money than anyone had expected and attracting large crowds. But I couldn't help thinking that now the soldiers were returning, surely women's football no longer had a place.

'Of course we are still needed,' Hettie replied sternly. 'There will still be injured servicemen coming home. There's still money to be raised.' She paused. 'And anyway, people like to watch our girls play – they are really popular now. I think there'd be riots if they stopped now!'

Flo nodded. 'That's true. I get stopped in the street all the time. People actually recognise me. Fancy that!'

'The Dick, Kerr Girls aren't going anywhere,' Alice said. 'The war might be over, but our journey has only just started.'

'That's good to know,' I replied, liking their spirit.

'You must be relieved,' Alice said, facing me. 'To see this war over. To finally put all this behind you.' She spread out her arms as if to indicate the fact. 'You can begin something new. Start over.'

I smiled back at her, even though it felt a bit false of me to do so. The last thing I could imagine at the moment was starting over.

'It really is an exciting time, any road,' I said finally.

But I meant for the Dick, Kerr Girls.

My future was far less exciting. What on earth was I going to do now?

I woke in the middle of the night feeling a hard, forceful pressure against my chest. Across the room, I could hear the gentle snores and murmurs from Martha and Hettie – but they seemed so far away somehow. I tried to move my legs, but it was as if there was a huge weight pressing me down, holding me still. I was sinking back into the bed. Cold, seeping sweat was drenching my skin and slipping down into my open mouth.

I blinked in the poor light. I closed my eyes and prayed for it to stop.

It was all too much.

'Ey up. Are you coming to the match today?' Hettie asked, looking at me hopefully.

We were all sitting in the kitchen having breakfast together – all apart from Dad, who had already left for work. In some ways it was a relief he wasn't there. Although Dad had been kind to me since my return, I hated how he flinched when he saw me limp, and the way his sad eyes skimmed over my face, showing how much he worried for me.

'Well, are you?' Hettie asked again, getting impatient.

My stomach felt like a heavy knotted mass. My head throbbed and I rubbed at it absently.

'I'm not sure,' I said. 'I might. I don't quite know yet.'

'I'll come,' Martha interrupted; the excitement was clear in her face. 'Can I come instead? I want to see the girls. You know I want to.'

'No, Martha, I need you to help at home,' Mam replied sternly. 'I can't have everyone leaving me here to do the chores.'

Martha returned to her porridge, her expression now sour. She knew it was never any use arguing with Mam.

Mam got to her feet and placed her cool hand on my brow, roughly pushing my hair aside. 'What's up, lad? Is it your leg? Is it troubling you still? Or is it something else? Does your head hurt?'

It did a bit, of course, but I didn't want to worry her. She'd only send me back up to bed. I realised that if I were to stay at home, I would probably be kept to my room all day, with Mam bringing me hot toddies to try and make me feel better. And then Dad would come home, and he'd worry even more.

'Go on then. I'll come to the game,' I said to Hettie finally, forcing a smile. 'I suppose the fresh air might do me good.'

Hettie smiled. 'I reckon it will. Bring your camera too. You might be able to take some photographs. Mr Frankland already said he would pay to develop them for you. He knows it can be expensive.'

Mr Frankland was Hettie's boss at the Dick, Kerr Factory; he'd also been mine for a time before the war. He was a very kind and intelligent man, with an ambitious streak. I think that's what made him want to manage the ladies football team at the factory in the first place. He had seen the potential in the girls and wanted to help them do even better.

When I'd first got home from the war, Hettie had told me tales of their first season playing, and how they had done extremely well – winning matches, gaining attention and filling the grounds they played in. People had started to talk more and more about this team of local lasses – a team as good as any men's team they had seen.

But, according to Hettie, Mr Frankland wanted more than just a few wins. He wanted to grow the team, to encourage more players to join and to expand the areas where they played. He wanted the team to be known throughout the country.

'It's a shame you won't be on the pitch,' I said to her. 'I would've loved to have seen that.'

I never got to see Hettie play, as I was away fighting while she was developing her skills, but according to some of the girls, she was quite a whizz on the wing.

'Oh, that doesn't matter,' Hettie said. 'There's so many better players on the team, you would only get bored if you were to watch me.'

I could hear the sadness in her voice though, saw how her eyes dipped away from mine. I felt for her. It was awful to have injuries that stopped you doing the things you wanted to.

'The most important thing is, I'm still part of building up the Dick, Kerr Girls to be even better,' Hettie said. 'You can be part of it too, Freddie. You can help document their journey with your photographs. It's such an exciting time.'

I nodded.

'And as they become more famous, who knows where it could all lead!' Hettie continued.

'Well – I suppose we'll have to see what will happen,' I said cautiously. 'Lots might change now.

The Dick, Kerr Girls might not be as popular once the men's games restart properly.'

'Oh, don't go thinking like that,' Hettie said quite sternly. 'The Dick, Kerr Girls are here to stay, just you wait and see.'

'I will.' I smiled at her.

I watched as Hettie got up from her seat, her eyes sparkling with excitement, her cheeks rosy and healthy. She really had grown up so much in such a short time. Hettie was no longer my cheeky little sister; she was a bright, strong girl with forthright opinions and views that couldn't be shifted.

And I hoped, for her sake more than anyone else's, that she was right and I was wrong.

The Dick, Kerr Girls were playing a team from the British Westinghouse factory in Manchester. The game was at Deepdale, the Dick, Kerr home ground, and Hettie happily reminded me that it would be the first peacetime match to be played there.

There was a different atmosphere in the stands today. Hettie had stayed with me, rather than taking her place alongside Mr Frankland on the sidelines. She huddled close, drawing an arm across her body.

'I'll sit with you today,' she said. 'It'll make a change.'

'Only if you're sure?' I replied, feeling secretly pleased. I wrapped my own arms tighter around me. It was good to have her company. It made me feel less alone.

'What we're doing is still so important,' she said, as the teams ran out on to the pitch. 'We need to raise money more than ever. The war may be over, but people's battles aren't. There is still so much we have to rebuild.'

I watched as the Dick, Kerr Girls warmed up. They all looked to be in good shape. Alice Kell in particular caught my eye. I knew she was one of the key players in the team, as well as being the captain. She was strong and fast and not afraid to shout instructions to her team.

I tapped my camera. 'I'm going to take some action shots, but it'll be nice to get a photo of Alice after the game.'

Hettie smiled. 'I'll take you over at the end. Hopefully we'll have something to celebrate!'

And indeed we did! The game itself was fast-moving, but also very much one-sided. Our girls tore through the Manchester Ladies' defence and left them looking quite ordinary.

I found myself jumping up and down on the spot, despite the pain in my leg, cheering the team on with scores of others. They had so much support here!

So many people were keen to see the girls do well.

It wasn't long before Flo Redford guided the ball into the top corner of the goal, showing a deft skill that most men would struggle to match. The crowd roared its approval. Then, just before half-time, she scored her second – picking up a nifty cross from Lily Jones and glancing the ball sweetly into the back of the net.

The half-time whistle blew and Hettie turned to me, grinning.

'They just get better and better, don't they?' she said. 'Mr Frankland really believes we can arrange games even further afield and raise more money for charity. Wouldn't that be wonderful?'

'They do seem unstoppable,' I admitted. Apart from one unexpected defeat early in the season, the girls' record was pretty much untarnished and Hettie had told me that when they'd lost, they'd still put up a good game.

The second half began pretty much as the last had ended. The Dick, Kerr Girls had total control, but this time it was Alice who shone. I watched in admiration as the fearless player dribbled and skipped her way past the unbalanced goalkeeper and slotted the ball into the back of the net.

3–0.

The crowd roared once again.

And then, just when we thought the final whistle would blow, a quick pass from Nellie Mitchell found Alice again, inside the box. She was being marked tightly by an opposing defender but with a quick turn, Alice managed to unbalance her marker and slip the ball neatly into the far corner. It was a peach of a goal. I yelled in approval.

The final whistle blew, and the girls threw their arms up in joy.

This might have been the first match since the war ended, but I quickly realised that the Dick, Kerr Girls weren't going anywhere. I liked the rush of excitement and joy I always felt while watching them. I didn't want that to go anywhere either.

Hettie and I quickly walked down to pitch-side and I took some photographs of the girls celebrating. Then Hettie called them together so that we could take an informal team photo of the girls all together. Hettie told me that the official team photograph was due to be taken in the new year, so this was another chance for me to practice.

The girls huddled together excitedly, looking very professional in their striped kits and neat caps. I watched as they straightened their socks and pulled down their crumpled tops to try and look smart.

'You need to take some more photos before the game,' Alice said brightly. 'We might not look so mucky then!'

'Make sure you get my good side,' Flo called, turning her face slightly to the left. 'I want to be seen looking my best.'

'You can take my photograph any way you chose,' another girl said with a laugh. 'My face'll probably crack the glass!'

I took the photographs as best I could, feeling quite nervous and bashful in front of these loud, outgoing women. I wasn't the most practised photographer in the world – I hadn't even had this camera for long – so I was worried that I might not do a very good job and the girls and Mr Frankland would be disappointed in me.

As if sensing this, Mr Frankland approached me and laid a hand on my shoulder.

'You can take your time, practise taking shots,' he said. 'You'll get more confident as you go, and we can only benefit from any photographs that mark our progress.'

'Thank you,' I said shyly. 'I only hope a few of these will be half-decent.'

'I'm sure they will be,' Mr Frankland replied. 'Now, let me share a secret with you, young Freddie.

What would you say if I told you I have my eye on a few new girls that could strengthen this side even further?'

'Really?' I said, immediately interested. 'Who are they?'

Mr Frankland simply tapped the side of his nose. 'You will see in time, son, but mark my words, they are very impressive. If you think this team is good now . . .' He drew in a deep breath. 'Well, just you wait.'

3

Johnnie was singing a few moments ago – some music hall song that I didn't recognise. His thick Yorkshire accent usually makes me smile, but Johnnie hasn't spoken for a while. I know his chest is hurting. He is struggling to stay merry.

I'd give anything to hear Johnnie sing again. For his lilting voice to lift the mood. It would help us, I'm sure. I could ask him, but I know that's too much. I wish we could just sing and talk and be silly again. It's all I want. I want him to talk to me about football, or his factory job, or his sweetheart at home. I want him to tell me all his wonderful stories again.

'We'll rest soon,' I say. My words are choked out. It's not up to me when we rest. My words are not a command, only a desperate hope.

Johnnie says nothing. I wonder if he can actually hear me.

'Soon . . .' I repeat. I lick my dry lips. I wonder how it's possible to keep fighting when you are so tired your legs do not feel like your own any more.

I turn to Johnnie. I see him wilt; his entire body sags. I see his arm tremble. He's so tired. We all are. I pull on his arm, helping him as he staggers in the soggy trench.

'I'll be all right, lad,' he says finally. His smile is weak. He rights himself and marches next to me. 'I'm tired, but I'll be all right.'

'Are you sure?'

'Of course.' His voice gains strength. 'We look after each other here, don't we?'

Johnnie had always looked after me. Always. But look how had I repaid him, on that final night. I'd let him down.

I pulled the blankets over my head and blinked back the tears. I didn't look after Johnnie. Not in the end.

I stumbled through the next few weeks. I tried not to make a big deal of how I was feeling, not wanting to alarm my family. Hettie knew I was still suffering with nightmares, after all, she shared a room with me. Some nights I found her sitting on the edge of my bed, stroking my arm or gently wiping my brow. I always shooed her away, telling her that I was all right and didn't need her fussing. I didn't want to be a burden to her.

As far as she was aware, I was just having silly dreams – it was nowt to be concerned about at all.

I watched her as she left for work each morning, bright as a button. I realised that the Dick, Kerr Factory had really changed her for the better. I remember when I left for war, she was quite a different girl then – so shy and reserved – but now a quiet confidence had taken over. She left the house quickly each day, excited to get to the office and to meet up with the other women on the way. I knew that they would talk in their breaks about the upcoming matches. I would give anything to feel that sort of excitement again – about anything.

Sometimes, when Dad was on a later shift, he'd be there in the mornings too. He'd fix me with a heavy stare over his morning paper. Most days he remained quiet, but there were other days when he chose to talk to me. These were far harder.

'That could be you too, lad, ' he said one time, after Hettie had left for the factory. 'Working there again. I'm sure Hettie could have a word with Mr Frankland and fix you up with something. A boy needs to work. It's not right otherwise.'

'I'm not sure, Dad . . .' I'd replied, dipping my gaze away from his. 'I still struggle to keep weight on my leg and . . .'

I hesitated. Dad's stare was very hard to bear. I knew that he too was in pain every day. He was involved in a tram accident years ago, which hurt his back badly. We all knew that the long hours on the docks tired him and made his pain worse, but he never complained. To him, it was just his life. He had to get on with it. I just didn't know if I was capable of the same.

My fingers had circled in the crumbs left on my plate. How could I tell my dad that it was more than the pain in my leg stopping me from going back to the Dick, Kerr factory? Just the thought of returning to that deafening, busy factory floor made my stomach twist in fright. I hated loud noises now, they took me right back to the front line of the war – to the gunfire and crashing sound of grenades as they exploded.

'Leave the boy alone,' Mam had said sternly. 'He'll go back to work when he's ready.'

'Well, let's hope that's sooner rather than later,' Dad said quietly. 'No good is had by skulking around the house feeling sorry for yourself. I'm worried, is all.'

I'd turned my face away, not wanting Dad to see the redness in my cheeks.

But the worst thing was knowing that Dad was worried about me.

I think I found that the hardest thing to deal with.

It was a crisp December morning and Martha and I were out in the yard. Martha was carefully moving my old football around the two jumpers I had laid on the ground. I'd already had her running up and down the ginnel by the side of our house. I was surprised at how agile and quick she was for her age. She really had come on so well.

'I've been practising, see!' she said proudly. 'I want a trial for the Dick, Kerr Girls. Hettie said I could.'

'Well, I can see an improvement from the clumsy kid I once played with,' I joked. 'Try it again, but this time with your left foot.'

Martha nodded and carefully positioned her body over the ball. I lifted the camera and took a picture of her moving swiftly between the makeshift cones. She had a natural grace about her.

'Hettie says I remind her of Flo,' Martha said, once she reached the end. 'She thinks I could be a forward like her.'

'I don't see why not, Marth.'

'Hettie says I'm too young to train with the girls, but I want to get bigger and stronger so that I can.'

She paused. 'You were a good footballer, weren't you? *Before—*'

She let the word hang between us. I instantly peered down at my gammy leg. Hidden under my trousers, you couldn't see there was much wrong, but the scar was long and ugly and the muscle was already beginning to wither away. I would always walk with a limp, a permanent reminder of my failings.

'I used to love football,' I replied softly. 'And yeah, I was rather good. And quick too, I'll have you know. I do miss it.'

'You can take me to the matches,' Martha said, her hands on her hips. 'Mam says I'm too young to go on my own. But I want to see the girls play; I want to learn.'

'Aren't you meant to be doing chores then?'

Martha grinned. It was her cheeky smile – her way of getting what she wanted from me. She usually succeeded. 'But if you tell Mam that you want to go, and you need me to keep you company . . .' She widened her eyes. 'Go on, Fred! Mam will let me if you say you want me with you. She knows that Hettie is always too busy with Mr Frankland and the team.'

I shrugged. 'Oh, all right. I don't see why not.'

'We can go to the Christmas Day match together,' Martha decided. 'They need to win that one, after the Lancaster Ladies game. They were so unlucky then.'

I nodded. 'Yeah. Why not. It'll be good to see them win again.' I was keen myself to see some of the new girls that Mr Frankland had already taken on. I hoped they were as good as Hettie had been saying.

Hettie had complained non-stop after the Lancaster game. I'd not seen it myself, but it had been a tight one by all accounts and apparently the Dick, Kerr girls had been unlucky to lose, narrowly missing many chances themselves.

'But Lancaster had some amazing players,' Hettie had confided to me. 'Jessie Walmsley, Jennie Harris and Annie Hastie. They all played a wonderful game. It really made a difference. Which is why it's such good news that Mr Frankland has persuaded two of them to join us!'

'Really?' I'd said, my interest growing. 'Which two?'

'Annie and Jennie at the moment. Isn't it great? They will both be playing their first game on Christmas Day against Bolton Ladies, isn't that wonderful?'

'It should strengthen the side,' I agreed, impressed that Mr Frankland had managed to bring the two women over.

'And the word is, Jessie Walmsley will be joining us soon too,' Hettie had added. 'Which is really good news. She's meant to be very skilful.'

It was only now, as I stood with Martha and remembered this conversation, that the name Jessie Walmsley came back to me. It had stood out to me at the time but then, I couldn't work out why.

Who was Jessie Walmsley?

The Christmas Day match was upon us before we knew it. Martha was more excited about the game than her stocking or Mam's home-made mince pies. She gulped her food down, barely taking the time to swallow, and was soon tugging on my arm to leave.

'Come on, Fred! We have to leave now if we're to get there in time so I can stand at the front and see properly.'

'All right,' I said, pulling on my coat. I felt a bit grumpy, wondering if Martha was making reference to my leg, which left me walking much slower than I used to.

'I'll walk with you,' Hettie said, pulling a scarf tightly round her neck. 'But I'll have to nip away when we get there. I want to see the girls before they play – wish them luck and all that. It's tradition.'

'You're so lucky,' Martha said. 'I want to see the girls too.'

'And you shall, one day,' Hettie soothed. 'One day, you might even be part of the team.'

'Not another one,' Dad grumbled behind his newspaper, but his tone was quite light-hearted. He'd had a sherry and he looked like he was ready to nap in this chair.

'Aren't you coming today, Dad?' Hettie asked.

He shook his head. 'I'm too tired, lass. You young ones go. Enjoy it.' His eyes raked over mine carefully. 'The fresh air might do you good.'

It won't magically fix me, I wanted to say, but I kept my mouth closed. Today wasn't the day for such discussions.

We walked briskly towards the Deepdale ground, or as briskly as we could with me in their company. I tried to ignore the pain in my leg and walked as quickly as I could manage. I hated slowing the girls down and resented the limp that I now had.

On the way, Hettie taught Martha a song that fans used to sing for the new player Jennie Harris when she was at Lancaster Ladies.

You've heard talk about professionals, that once got
a rattling wage

But I will mention still another one, who is marked
　　on history's page,
To play the game called football you would scarce
　　believe your eyes
So just drop down to Lancaster, it will take you by
　　surprise.
To see a bonnie lassie, friends, by gum she's earning
　　fame
She plays for the Projectiles and Jennie Harris is her
　　name.
She really is a marvel and astonishes the crowd
For when she scores a brilliant goal, the spectators
　　shout so loud.
You would think the heavens opened when Jennie
　　does appear
For her dribbling down at Preston caused many a
　　hearty cheer.
The toffs they do admire her, left their ladies in
　　fine style
To fall in love with Jennie, the little wrench from
　　the Projectiles.

Martha soon picked it up and especially liked the last
line, which she sung with particular glee.

'One day the crowd will sing about me,' she declared. 'The little wrench from Preston North End.'

Hettie rubbed Martha's hair. 'Why not, Marth, anything is possible. It's good to dream big.' She paused. 'But it means that you have to work particularly hard if you want to play for a good team.'

'I will,' Martha replied. 'I really will.'

At the ground, Hettie kissed us both on the cheek and scuttled off to find the girls. I could see she was buzzing with both anticipation and concern.

'I hope the girls do well today,' I said to Martha, as we eased through the crowd. 'It always upsets Hettie when they don't.'

'She says they're her second family,' Martha replied. 'So, I suppose it would make her feel bad if they didn't win.'

Luckily, we managed to find a spot at the front by the halfway line. Martha was very impressed and gripped the rail, leaning forward all the time to see if she could spot the girls first.

'I can't see them yet . . . I want to see Jennie Harris. I'm going to sing her song. I wonder if she'll hear me? I can't see her yet . . . where are they . . . Oh!'

Her voice was taken by the sudden sight of the girls running out on to the pitch. I had to admit, every time

I saw them, I was always taken by how smart and professional they looked in their neat black-and-white kit. Behind me the crowd surged a bit and then there was a gentle ripple of applause, building like a wave.

'C'mon girls,' said a rough voice behind me. 'You show the Bolton lot what you're made of.'

Martha was leaning further forward, her cheeks flushed with excitement. 'There's Jennie, I can see her now. Oh, isn't she dainty! I think she might be my favourite.'

The girls took their positions, and the referee blew the whistle. Soon, I was swept up in the excitement of the game. All thoughts of my leg, of my dark, heavy nightmares, of Johnnie even, were pushed aside. My mind suddenly cleared.

For ninety wonderful minutes I could stand with my little sister and be taken somewhere else – somewhere quite different, almost magical.

Hettie was right. Watching the Dick, Kerr Girls was not only thrilling, it was addictive. I didn't want it to end. I wanted to be here, in this stand, cheering the girls on for ever. It was quite a feeling.

The game itself was played at remarkable speed and although the Bolton Ladies took an early lead, our girl,

Molly Walker, managed to secure an equaliser before half-time. I thought both Martha and I would lose our voices because we cheered so much.

After the break, Bolton took the lead once more, but it wasn't long before Dick, Kerr's Nellie Mitchell equalised again, after receiving a wonderful cross from Molly Walker and placing it squarely in the back of the net.

The result was 2–2. A draw. But it had been the most exhilarating game. All the Dick, Kerr girls had played a part and worked well as a team and it was exciting to think what they might be capable of in the future. Surely, they were only going to get better?

But really, the score itself was irrelevant. As I looked at Martha's flushed and happy face, and felt my own heart thundering in my chest, I knew this game had been about much more than a simple win.

It had also been about finding some feeling of belonging again.

4

''Ere, Freddie, on my head son!'

I lob the ball over and it lands perfectly, as Johnnie jumps up to meet it. He glances his head to the side and we watch as the ball sails wonderfully through the air, flying gracefully between our makeshift goal posts – two battered billy cans.

'Yes!' Johnnie pumps the air and runs around cheering. Some of the lads laugh with us, but a couple of the older ones, huddled close, shoot us cross looks.

'Watch out, boys! This is no time for high jinks!'

Johnny ignores them, instead tugging at my arm, beckoning at me to sit with him for a moment. His breath is ragged and his cheeks are pink. I don't think I've seen him look so alive.

'God, I miss playing,' he says, reaching for his cup. I know he has rum in it. Like many of the lads here, he drinks it to steady his nerves. But I don't like the taste, it makes my tongue and throat burn.

'I do, too,' I admit, crouching beside him. 'And watching the matches back at home.'

Johnnie nods slowly. 'It were a Saturday treat that – going down to the game, cheering on the boys. Not a care in the world.' He shook his head slowly and whistled. 'Not long, lad, and we will be back there. Football, all of that ...'

'Do you think? I hope so, Johnnie. I miss it.'

I reach inside my pocket. As usual, my stomach is raw with hunger, but I know I have some bully beef left to eat. How I miss Mam's home-cooked dinners – hotpot, roast dinner. By gum, I even miss her tripe.

Johnnie peers down at me, his eyes glistening in the weakening light.

'We will get back there soon, lad. Back home. I can promise you that.'

I shake my head. 'You can't know that, Johnnie. Not for certain. You know how bad it is now.' I shiver, thinking of the men we've already lost. The ghosts of the fallen soldiers still linger among us.

His hand rests briefly on my shoulder, his voice lowers.

'Oh, I do know. You'll get back. You have to keep believing that. Promise me, lad.'

I chuckle, feeling a little uneasy. 'All right Johnnie, all right. I promise. There's no need to get all serious on me.'

He sits back, a soft laugh escapes him. 'You're right, Freddie. I'm being too serious. There's no need for that, eh?'

He gestures to my food. '*Eat up, we can have another kick around before it gets late.*'

I eat, trying to ignore how tasteless the meat is in my mouth and how Johnnie's gaze seems to be drifting some place else, somewhere far away.

'*We need to have fun while we still can,*' *he says quietly.*

This time I do not reply.

Mr Frankland had gathered the girls together on the Deepdale field. It was a week day, after work, and although many of the girls looked quite tired, they still looked smart and clean for their official team photograph. An excited murmur passed through them as I approached awkwardly with the camera. I waved and tried to busy myself getting my equipment ready. I had already taken some practice shots before, so this should have been easy for me – but the anxiety still gnawed deep in my stomach. What if I messed this up? This was to be a key photograph for the team and I wanted to get it right for them.

'It's important the girls feel relaxed and happy,' Mr Frankland explained. 'Besides, I have no doubt that you will do an excellent job. I saw the previous photographs you took, when I got them developed. They were very good.'

Hettie had brought some of the pictures home to show me. I could see that she was quite impressed with what I had done.

'Look at this one of Alice,' she said, pointing. 'It's so natural; you really caught her smile. And in this one, our Flo looks grand!'

I had to admit, I had felt a surge of pride looking at those photographs. Really, they had just been test shots to get me used to working with the girls and get used to the camera, but even I had to admit that they looked far better than simple practice shots. It was quite satisfying seeing the strength and beauty of these girls, frozen in perfect images – and just as satisfying to know I had taken them.

But the team photograph today was far more important. This would properly tell everyone who the Dick, Kerr Girls were. It was also an opportunity for the new team members to be officially included for the first time.

I saw Jennie Harris straight away, as she took her place on the seated bench. Annie Hastie was standing behind – a tall girl with short dark curls and a cheeky smile, Annie was hard to miss. But then my eyes fell on someone else. Another girl approaching the back line, who greeted Annie warmly before taking her place for the shot. She was as tall as Annie but slightly stockier, with a bright smile that was immediately infectious and made me want to smile back. Her short brown curls tumbled out of her neat cap and what looked like a scar marked one side of her face. She caught my eye and nodded slightly. I quickly realised who she was.

Jessie Walmsley. Of course. So she had joined after all.

I also remembered where I had heard her name before.

It had been at the Moor Park military hospital.

One particular morning, I started hearing whispers between soldiers and noticed knowing looks being flashed between the staff. It was clear something big had recently happened, but I wasn't quite sure what. I decided to approach one of the more friendly nurses about it.

'Oh! We're not meant to talk about it,' she said, after a little persuasion. 'The whole thing wasn't allowed to be reported or anything, but it was truly awful.'

'You can tell me,' I insisted, switching on what I hoped was my best trustworthy look. 'I won't tell a soul, I promise.'

The nurse was very young, and I think keen to impress. She sat herself on the end of my bed and leant towards me a little. 'You promise not to breathe a word?'

'Cross my heart,' I said, drawing my hand across my chest.

She nodded. 'All right then. Well, you know The National Projectile Factory over in White Lund? It exploded! There was a terrible fire. They say that shrapnel from the factory was sent in all directions and all the homes nearby were evacuated.'

'That is awful,' I said. 'Why wasn't it reported?'

'Well, I'm told because of national security concerns.' The nurse leant in closer, whispering now. 'We don't want the enemy to know our weaknesses, do we? Where would that leave us?'

I flinched. 'No, we certainly don't.' I pulled myself up straighter in the bed, trying to ignore the stiffness and resistance in my body. 'How many died?'

'Oh, I'm not sure. I heard ten were recovered from the ruins. There was a young lass hurt in the explosion too. I know of her – she's friends with my sister. Her name's Jessie Walmsley.'

'Oh, the poor thing. Is she recovered now?'

'She was scarred. On her cheek. But she'll pull through; she's a true Lancaster lass and full of grit. As a child she had the misfortune to be struck by lightning.

Who could imagine such a thing? She was lucky to survive that. She's a special girl, is Jessie Walmsley.'

And now here Jessie was, right in front of me, the newest member of the Dick, Kerr team.

How strange fate was at times.

Hettie was approaching me, a small frown etched on her face.

'What's that, Freddie?' she asked.

I realised I must have said Jessie's name out loud. I felt my cheeks heat up.

'Jessie . . . I was just thinking how I had heard a little about her before, at the hospital.' I paused. 'I was told she's very special.'

Hettie's smile widened. 'Oh, she is. Aren't we lucky to have her?' Her voice dropped a little. 'She doesn't like to talk about what happened to her, though. She doesn't like the fuss. She's such a humble lass.'

'And so happy.' I watched as she continued to laugh and joke with the girls as they took their remaining places.

'She is,' Hettie agreed. 'She will be so good for the team.'

I took a series of shots in the afternoon light. The girls arranged themselves quickly – some seated on the front bench with their arms folded and the others standing behind, tall and proud. Girls like Emily Jones, Nellie Mitchell and Jennie Harris smiled shyly for the camera, whilst others such as Annie Hastie and Lily Jones had more formal expressions. And Jessie? She had a twinkle in her eye that really caught my attention. I found myself grinning back at her, my earlier anxiety disappearing.

Mr Frankland came over once I had finished and clapped me on the back. Hettie had already left me to join the girls now that they could relax again. I could see her laughing and joking with Alice and Flo.

'Well done, lad. I can't wait to see the result,' Mr Frankland said. 'What a fine-looking team, eh?'

'They certainly are,' I agreed.

'Have you met our new players?' he asked. 'I told you I had my eye on a few of these before. I'm so pleased we managed to coax them all over.'

'I've not had a chance to meet them yet, sir. I've been too busy setting myself up.'

'I'd not bother with that nonsense of calling me sir,' he said in a jovial way. 'How long have you known me for? You worked with me long enough before the blessed war and your dear sister is like a daughter to me now. I insist on Alfred, or, if you must, Mr Frankland.'

'Thank you . . .' I hesitated. 'Mr Frankland.'

Calling Mr Frankland by his first name seemed rather too informal; I wasn't sure Dad would agree with that. He was always reminding us to watch our place.

'Ah, Jessie lass! We were just talking about you!' A group of the girls were now approaching us, laughing brightly and adjusting their caps as if they had just been out on the town dancing. Mr Frankland hooked his arm around Jessie and drew her close. 'Meet Freddie. He's our Hettie's brother. He will be with us quite a bit this season, taking photographs of the team whenever he can.'

Jessie turned to face me. Closer up, I could clearly see the raised scar on the left side of her face, but she didn't seem at all self-conscious about it. I suppose it wasn't awfully uncommon now. I knew that a lot of the women at the Dick, Kerr factory had been injured while working with explosives. Hettie spoke about it often and always worried that something awful like that would happen to someone she knew.

Jessie's eyes widened as she looked me up and down, and that wonderful smile of hers stretched further across her face. The other girls giggled and moved away.

'Ow do, Freddie,' she said, holding out her hand in greeting. 'It's good to meet you. I've already been introduced to Hettie several times now and she's grand, so if you're anything like her . . .'

'Well, I try my best.' I smiled.

'Hettie did mention you,' she said. 'You were at the Front, weren't you? Injured in battle?'

My hand fluttered by my useless leg. 'Yes. My leg took a hammering, and my head and lungs too, although they're not so bad now. I guess I got my share.'

'Were you at Moor Park hospital after?' she asked. 'I know people who work there.'

'Yes, yes I was.' I paused. 'I actually knew a nurse there who knows you.'

'Really?' She blushed a little. 'I'm not sure there's much to know.'

Her smile was still on her lips, but it had lessened a little.

'I'm so sorry about your injuries. My younger brother died you know, in the war. In 1914. It killed my family in many ways. I've seen the true extent of what war can do. It's awful.'

I nodded. 'It is.'

'Jessie is a most brilliant footballer,' Mr Frankland interjected. 'Probably helped by having a big family, eh? You can learn all sorts that way.'

Jessie's grin was back. 'I've loved football for as long as I can remember. It's as much a part of me as my own blood. I'm so excited to be part of the Dick, Kerr Girls. Everyone in these parts is talking about them. It feels like I'm joining at such a good time.'

'It really is,' Mr Frankland agreed. 'Especially now we have you on board, Jessie. Not only a fine player, but a local hero too. Did you hear about her, Freddie? Did you hear what she did?'

I straightened up. 'I heard about the explosion and that Jessie was there.' My eyes lingered on her face. I noticed how pink her cheeks suddenly were.

Jessie flapped us both away. 'It were nowt. Anyone would've done the same in my situation.'

'It was hardly nowt, Jessie!' Mr Frankland boomed. 'You're considered a true hero around these parts. You—'

'No, please don't.' Jessie held up her hand. 'Please, Mr Frankland, I'd rather you didn't bring it all up now. I find it a bit much.'

He shrugged. 'Of course, Jessie. I don't like to upset you. I just thought Freddie here would want to hear what you did.'

'Well, I'm sure he doesn't want to be bored to tears by my life stories.' Jessie dipped her head away from both of us. 'It really was nothing. You don't need to make a fuss.'

I waited for a moment or two and then spoke.

'To be honest, I feel much the same when people ask me about the war. It always makes me feel a bit uncomfortable and unsure. I don't like being called a hero, even though complete strangers insist on it.'

'Well, I for one like to applaud bravery and courage,' Mr Frankland said firmly. 'But I understand that you don't want your details broadcast everywhere, Jessie. I must learn to have more discretion.' He coughed lightly.

'It really is nothing,' Jessie repeated, looking quite shy. 'But it's been lovely to meet you, Freddie. I really hope we get the chance to chat again.'

'Me too,' I agreed heartily. 'I would like that very much.'

And I meant it.

I realised that for the first time since returning from war, I'd met someone who helped my mood lift. Someone with a smile that could warm me from inside out.

I had a feeling I was going to really like Jessie Walmsley.

5

We are resting again between battles. Johnnie is always the loud one, making us all laugh with his funny jokes and songs. I'm standing back, watching. I observe as Johnnie moves around the group, slapping men on the shoulders and geeing them on. He talks easily, telling us about his beautiful young wife, his young baby at home.

He's older than me and you can still easily tell. He holds himself tall, despite his short stature. He turns his nose up at the Germans. He's not scared. I don't think Johnnie is scared of anything and if he is, he doesn't show it. Not like me. Fear shows on my face as plain as my nose. I cannot hide it.

He comes towards me with his easy swagger. He throws an arm over my shoulder. His grin is lazy and slightly lopsided. His chestnut-brown hair falls into one eye.

'Freddie,' he says brightly. 'Don't look so scared. It'll be all right, you know. We're all in this together.'

The others reply, cat-calling, holding up their tin mugs towards me in a mock cheer.

The air around me is unfamiliar and stale. The earth is spongy and wet beneath us. In the distance, I can hear the boom of gunfire. It never seems to stop. Each blast rattles through my body and ignites another blaze of fear within me.

I hate it here. I want to go home.

No one here can know that.

But Johnnie doesn't see me that way.

He calls me his brother.

He grips my shoulder, squeezes it reassuringly. 'Everything will be all right,' he says again. 'As long as we look after each other. We look after our brothers in arms – our family – and we'll be all right.'

And in that moment, I believe him. I really do.

'Who is Johnnie?'

Hettie and I were sitting on the small wall outside the house, watching Martha play football with the boys from the street again. Up until Hettie's question, I had been feeling in a good mood.

'He's a solider from my regiment,' I replied quietly. 'Why?'

'You call his name sometimes at night – I wondered whether he . . .'

Hettie paused, chewed briefly on her lip. She looked

up at me and I think she saw something in my face. Or perhaps I flinched without realising, but luckily she didn't finish her question. I was relieved. The last thing I needed to do was talk about Johnnie now. He was already taking over my nights, and I didn't want him taking over my days as well.

'The dreams are rotten,' I said instead. 'But the doctors hope they will ease soon. They think in time they will stop altogether.'

'That's good,' Hettie said. 'They certainly seem to upset you.'

In front of us, Martha was running with the ball. Despite wearing a long dress and clumsy old boots, she was moving with speed and grace, nipping past one older, lankier lad quite easily and leaving him off balance. In fact, she made him look quite silly. The boy, obviously not liking that, smacked the floor in frustration.

'Go on, Marth!' Hettie called out to her proudly. 'Score one for us girls!'

Without pausing, Martha moved the heavy leather ball to her left foot and then, with a burst of energy, drove a shot between the makeshift tin-can goal. She immediately threw up her arms and whooped in delight. The older boy who she had wrong-footed scowled at her.

'That was a lucky shot,' he said.

'It was not,' Martha sang back. 'I got right around you and you know it.'

Some of the other lads on the street, including brothers Ronnie and Davey Marshall, nudged each other. They had played with Martha for long enough to know how good she was. The older boy walked over to another group of boys that looked the same age as him. None of them seemed happy. I wondered why Martha had agreed to play football with them if they were such bad losers.

'Martha is better than most of the lads around here,' Ronnie said. 'You better get used to it, Alfie.'

But this Alfie lad still didn't look impressed and his scowl only deepened further.

'It's not right, girls playing football. They're not designed for such things. My dad told me that.'

Hettie immediately sat up straighter. I swear I could feel the heat in her face.

'Eh? What exactly does your dad say, Alfie?' she asked.

Alfie turned to face us, probably realising for the first time that we were there. He was a skinny boy with a long, sad-looking face and a thatch of scruffy dirty-blonde hair decorating his large head. I think he was about fifteen or sixteen and I knew he lived at the end of the road with his father – a large, overweight, angry-looking man who wasn't exactly the friendliest sort.

'My dad says that women have been getting funny ideas,' Alfie said, his eyes fixed on Hettie. 'During the war they helped out, which was all well and good, but now they think they can just carry on—'

'And why can't they?' Hettie jumped in.

He scoffed. 'Because that's not how it should be.' His eyes glinted. 'It's not how things are ever meant to be. What would happen if all women thought they could act like men, eh? It's bad enough some of them are doing our jobs. Now we've got that bunch that want equal votes too . . .'

'The suffragettes,' Hettie said evenly. 'What those women are doing is amazing. I don't understand why you're being such a noddy.'

Alfie's face was getting red. 'I'm no noddy,' he spluttered.

'Yeah, you are,' Martha called back.

He turned to me and his expression brightened a little. 'Hey – you get it, don't you?' he said. 'You fought in the war? I saw you go off in your uniform. You know what it's like for us lads. It's different for us. It always will be.'

But what is *it like for us lads, Alfie?* I almost laughed in his face. I could see in this boy's expression the same bright-eyed patriotic hope I had felt going off to war. I had truly believed that I was doing some wonderful, adventurous thing – that the war would make me stronger, fitter, more worthy. That I would come home different somehow. That war might fix the problems inside of me.

But what had been the reality? Cold, wet mud. Gunfire and screams. Blood and guts. Tears and pain.

It hadn't fixed any problems, it had just caused even more!

'I think,' I said slowly. 'That there's little difference between lads and lasses. Not any more.'

Alfie shook his head at me. 'My dad said lads like you are weak. Your heads have gone all soft.'

I half-laughed. 'Maybe your dad's the weak one for not accepting things are really changing.' I paused. 'Or maybe he's like you, and is just scared because he knows he will be easily beaten by a girl.'

'Right!' Alfie went to charge for me, his fists raised.

I jumped off the wall, flinching as the pain flared up my leg. I didn't care that he wanted to punch me. I didn't fear his fist against my face, because nothing would hurt as much as the thoughts inside my head.

But as Alfie drew close to me, one of his friends dragged him away.

'Leave him, Alfie,' the boy said loudly. 'He got injured in the war. He can't walk properly, I've seen him. You can't go around hitting a cripple.'

Alfie's expression changed. He no longer looked angry, instead pity danced in his eyes.

'Oh,' he said, dropping his fists. 'I didn't realise. Maybe you took a knock to the head too, eh? Maybe that's what's making you act all strange?'

I stared at him coldly. 'I don't think so.'

His smile was sly, his eyes still fixed on mine. 'Well, something must've happened to you,' he said. 'To make you turn on your own kind.'

That night as I sat at the dinner table, thoughts of the earlier set-to were still churning in my head. Was Alfie right? Was I turning on my own kind?

Dad frowned at me, one bushy eyebrow lifted up in suspicion.

'Am I eating with my mouth open or something, lad?'

'No, sorry. I was just thinking.'

He swiped a large hand across his face. 'Reckon you do too much of that now – thinking. There's no time for that. Like I keep saying, you need to get yourself a job. It might stop your brain from overworking.'

'He's still recovering,' Mam scolded from across the table. 'Give the poor boy a break.'

'Aye, I understand that,' Dad said softly. 'I'm only saying that a job might help. The lad needs a distraction. Something to take his mind off his own thoughts. God knows, I know what that's like.'

'Freddie is helping us,' Hettie said quickly. 'He's taking our photographs, remember.'

'Aye.' Dad swiped at his potato, his forehead creasing. 'And that's all well and good, but taking pictures is just a hobby, isn't it? It's not substantial. The lad needs something more.'

I coughed awkwardly. 'I'm hoping that the experience will do some good. Maybe it'll help me get a job later down the line doing something similar. I'd like that.'

'Oh, you would, would you?' He stared at me, unblinking. Then his expression softened a little. 'Well, I'm sure you know best, son. I'm just making suggestions, that's all. I want what's best for you. I know you can't take on too much.'

'There's a job going at the grocers,' Mam said quietly. 'It's only a few hours a week, but they need someone to help behind the counter. Mrs Dawson was only talking about it the other morning.'

Dad turned away from me. 'Well, surely even our Freddie could manage that?'

I felt my skin heat up. I knew he was trying to be kind, but his words still stung.

'I'll go in tomorrow,' I said finally. 'I'll have a word. Maybe it'll be something to tide me over.'

Underneath the table, Hettie's hand snaked across to my lap. She squeezed my knee. 'Mrs Dawson is nice,' she said. 'You'll like it in there.'

'Yeah, maybe . . .' I replied.

Working for Mrs Dawson would bring in a bit of extra money to help Mam, but it wasn't what I really wanted to do. For a little while now, the tiniest glimmer of a dream had been building in me, that maybe my camera could be my way out of everything? But what was the point in speaking dreams out loud? That never helped anyone.

It was best to remain silent for now.

I put my knife and fork down. My dinner was only half eaten but suddenly I was no longer hungry.

Later, in our bedroom, Hettie sat on my bed and nudged me gently.

'Dad is trying his best,' she said. 'He worries about you. He really thinks going back to work will fix you.'

'Fix me?' I blinked back at her. 'I wasn't aware that I needed fixing?'

'Oh, Freddie.' She sighed and then threaded her arm over my shoulder, drawing me close. I could smell the sweet scent of her lavender soap and Mam's washing powder. 'It's not that you need fixing so much, but I think it's more like a part of you seems to be missing. The old Freddie is gone. The light-hearted one who laughed at everything and believed he could achieve anything he set his mind to. Do you remember him? Oh, how we loved him so.'

I lowered my head. I did remember him.

'I loved him too,' I whispered.

'It seems that since you've come back home from the hospital, you're drawing into yourself more. Instead of getting better . . . well, you're not.'

'I'm trying, our kid,' I said. 'It's hard being back here.

I'm reminded of how things were and how it's not the same for me now. It never can be.'

'I get that, Freddie, I do.' She squeezed me tighter. 'But we have a new future now. We have so much to look forward to, we really do.'

6

There was a storm and my clothes got soaked through. Now they have dried against me, hard and stiff like cardboard. My feet are blistered, and one heel is an open, oozing wound that I can feel split further with every movement. I haven't slept in so long I can't even remember. When I blink, the landscape blurs and bleeds into nothingness and I struggle to make sense of where we actually are.

'C'mon, Freddie,' Johnnie says. 'Head up. We've had our orders.'

I clasp the heavy gun in my hand, but my fingers are numb. I fear I may drop it at any moment. In fact, I fear I might myself collapse into a heap. I wonder if that would be such a bad thing? I could curl up in the mud and close my eyes. I could wait for this all to be over. I slump forward.

Somewhere, in the far distance, there are shouts and cries. The distant rumble of gunfire. The terror that I once felt has trickled away. I've become immune to these sounds.

I guess it would have been pretty here once – fresh, crisp grass and large sweeping trees – but now everything is dead or dying. The earth is collapsing beneath us. All beauty is gone.

I could be anywhere.

I could be in hell.

'I can't.' My voice feels small. I'm so tired, so very tired.

I think of home. Of my bed. Of my sisters' loud voices clattering into the room. I think of all the things I love and miss, and a hole opens up inside of me. It makes me feel light, like I could float away.

His hand grips me tighter. He tugs, forcefully. 'You're tired, that's all. Tired and hysterical. We'll be resting soon. You'll feel better. You can't stop. I'll not let you get into trouble.'

'I can't,' I repeat again, the words heavy in my mouth. 'Leave me.'

'You can!' He shouts now. 'On your feet, right now, or I swear I'll shoot you with this thing myself!'

He swings his gun in front of me. I've not seen Johnnie's face so tight with rage like this, his eyes glinting in the gloom.

So, I do what he says.

Slowly. Painfully. I get to my feet.

Martha and I were becoming regulars at Deepdale. We watched the first game of the new year against Bolton and were both glad to see Jessie impress the crowd with her quick feet and skills. The game itself ended in a draw, but everyone was in good spirits and excited to see the new line-up. I couldn't deny that the girls were looking a more solid side.

At the end of the month, we stood in the freezing January air to watch the girls take on the Heywood Ladies. This match was a bit tougher to watch, especially as the cold seemed to seep into my bones and made my leg feel heavy and head throb more than usual. But I couldn't be mardy about it when I had Martha next to me, who took delight at every kick and shot.

'They look great,' she said, eagerly leaning over the rail so that she could see more. 'And Alice Kell is back to fitness. You can tell. Look at her move. She's so fast.'

'She certainly looks good,' I agreed, but my eyes were on Jessie, who once again was having a grand game. 'That Walmsley girl is so strong. She seems to get around the other players so easily.'

The game was a fast one. Martha shrieked with joy as the first goal rocketed in, a lovely chip by the rejuvenated Alice. Flo scored two more before the half-time whistle, by which time Martha was almost beside herself.

'One day, that'll be me, Freddie. I'm telling you!' she said, pointing down at the pitch. 'I can make it happen all by myself, right?'

I felt a sudden stab of guilt.

'I only wish I could help you more,' I muttered. 'I know a lot of the girls practise with their older brothers and what good am I to you? I can barely kick the ball now . . .'

Martha's hand carefully landed on mine. 'Never mind that, Freddie. It doesn't matter. I get plenty of practice with the lads in our street.'

'I know, but even so . . .'

The second half started as the last had ended. Our girls were commanding in the midfield and soon scored a third goal courtesy of Lily Jones, who made an impressive run down the wing. The Heywood Ladies managed to claw one goal back, but it was far too late as Alice and then, I was glad to see, Jessie, picked up two more.

The end result was 5–1. The Deepdale crowd cheered once again, clearly pleased with what they'd seen.

Behind me, I heard a man talking to his friend.

'This team is better than most I've seen lately.

Have you heard the rumours? Apparently, they will be travelling further afield soon.'

'God help their opponents, then,' the friend replied. 'Because I reckon these girls could take anyone on and beat them. They really are unstoppable.'

I smiled in agreement. I couldn't help but think he was dead right.

I took some photographs after the game, while Martha went home with Hettie, keen to practise some of the skills she had just seen on the streets outside our home. I felt sorry for the lads – she'd soon be wearing them out!

The girls were used to having me around now, and they struck up positions as easily and naturally as if they were still playing a match. The next step would be to actually take some shots of a game, which Mr Frankland wanted me to do as soon as possible, now I was more confident with the camera.

'With any luck, we will be having photographs taken all the time,' Mr Frankland said, once I had finished. 'I want the girls' faces on every back page of the newspapers.'

'Have you got games planned further afield?' I asked. 'I heard some of the fans talking about it today.'

He nodded briskly. 'Indeed. I'm in talks with quite a few clubs. Hettie will be able to tell you more soon.' He patted my arm. 'And we want you there, recording the journey.'

'I'd love that.'

He took the camera from me carefully. 'I'll get these pictures developed then. I'm looking forward to seeing them.'

'Thank you.'

I was glad that Mr Frankland was doing this for me. I knew the local chemist developed the photographs, but it was very expensive – more than I could afford. One day, I would very much like to have a dark room of my own. I pictured how it would look, with dark, wet negatives strung up high from the ceiling. The sharp scent of chemicals flooding the space. The whole idea gave me a warm glow inside.

'You look miles away, Freddie,' Mr Frankland said. 'Are you all right?'

I flapped my hand. 'Oh, it's nothing much. I was just dreaming. That's all.'

'Dreams are good, lad. They give you something to focus on.'

'Maybe. Even so, I need to turn my mind to other

things now. Dreams are all well and good, but I need to think about getting an actual job now that I'm home.'

'Ah.' Mr Frankland breathed out softly. 'Have you any idea what you'd like to do?'

'Not really. I mean, I'd love to carry on taking photos, but there's not much to be made there.' I caught Mr Frankland's eye and blushed a little. 'Not that I'm not grateful for this experience and all.'

'Oh, I understand, lad.' He gestured at my camera. 'This is just to help you get back on your feet. I understand you might need a proper job. I only wish I could help you more. There's work at the factory of course. I could put in a word for you. I know you worked hard there before, but you'd be on your feet all day. It'll be tiring.'

He glanced at my leg. He didn't need to say anything more.

'Is there any work going in your office?'

He sighed gently. 'Not now, son. Albert is back from service now and your sister is doing such a fine job, I couldn't let her go. I don't have enough work for anyone else at the moment.'

'That's all right. I understand. Really, I do.'

I would have to go the grocers tomorrow and have

a word with Mrs Dawson, like Mam said. It wasn't the ideal solution and by gum, it wasn't a job I dreamt of doing, but at least it was something and I knew I would be lucky to find any work at the moment. I just hoped Mrs Dawson didn't expect me to do grocery deliveries. I wasn't sure that my leg would be strong enough to ride a bike.

'I'm sorry, son,' Mr Frankland said gently, breaking my train of thought. 'I'm sure something will come up.' He held the camera aloft. 'And you can keep doing this in the meantime, can't you? You never know where this all might lead.'

I smiled bitterly. 'Yeah – you never know.'

As Mr Frankland left me, his head nodding as if he were agreeing with the thoughts inside his own mind, I became aware of someone walking towards us. As usual, a bright, wide smile lit up her face. It was hard not to be cheered by the sight.

'Ow do, Jessie,' I said.

'All right, Freddie,' she said, a little shyly. 'Did you enjoy the game earlier?'

'I did. You all played very well.' I swallowed. 'Especially you, Jessie. You were superb in midfield.'

Jessie's eyes glowed, but she playfully batted me

away. 'Aw, don't be daft. I was nowt special. The other girls were amazing though. What a team, eh?'

I was impressed by how humble she was. This was the second time I had seen evidence of it. Jessie obviously wasn't someone who suffered from a big ego.

'My little sister Martha was watching too. She loves the team. She wants to be part of it one day.'

'Oh, I hope she does, Freddie. You'll have to introduce me to her next time.' Jessie paused; her eyes were fixed on mine. 'Freddie, I hope you don't mind, but I overheard your conversation with Mr Frankland just now . . .'

'What, about . . .' I floundered, feeling suddenly embarrassed. 'Oh, that was nothing. I just need to sort myself out with some work, that's all.'

'But I'm guessing that won't be easy, will it? After what you've been through?'

Something shone behind her gaze. I couldn't quite place it, but it was like she could see right through me. Could it be that she recognised the pain I was feeling? Was that even possible?

'I'll be fine,' I replied briskly. 'I can get some work at the local grocers. It's not perfect, but—'

'I might be able to help,' she interrupted, placing a slender hand on my arm. 'I can't promise anything, but I have a possible idea. Will you let me look into something for you? My fiancé may know someone who might be able to help.'

I shrugged. 'Of course.'

'Like I said, I can make no promises, but let me see what I can do.'

I nodded. I understood. People were often trying to help, by offering little 'jobs' and 'errands' for us injured servicemen to do and just as often it was inappropriate or came to nothing at all. But I didn't want to offend Jessie. She obviously meant well.

And, like Mr Frankland said, I didn't know where it might lead . . .

Some nights I lie in my bed, staring at the ghostly swirls on the ceiling, praying for morning to come. No sleep means my brain cannot shut down at all. No sleep means endless hours of tossing disturbed thoughts around in my head. No sleep means that the day will be so much harder, knowing that my body will be more sluggish and my mind much slower. I honestly don't know any more what's worst – the cruel dreams or the unending silence.

Tonight, I get up. I creep out of the bedroom so as not to wake my sleeping sisters. I slip out of the door, avoiding the creaking floorboard just outside. My parents sleep downstairs. As I hover on the top step, I can hear my dad's heavy snores rumbling in the darkness. I wonder how it is that he sleeps so easy.

I slip down the stairs slowly, praying that my tread does not reveal me. Carefully, I move into the kitchen. It is a cold room and the slate floor is icy under my feet. I do not care.

I move towards the window and stand silently.

From here, I can see out into our tiny yard. It's dark, of course. Inky shadows criss-cross the paved square. I can dimly make out Mam's washing line and the brick outhouse behind.

This is all so familiar to me. I have lived here all my life and yet, in the gloom, it looks so different. The darkness takes the sharp edges off everything; I feel like I'm looking at a smudged, dream-like memory of my past.

I can picture myself, from before, playing football in this yard with Hettie. I taught her all the tricks I knew. We would laugh and have such fun, running up and down the ginnel, out towards the street. Everything was so different then. It was so innocent.

It's not the same now. I really want it to be, but it's not.

I have changed.

This place has changed.

But what scares me most is now the country is starting to heal. It's starting to move on, as it rightly should.

But what if I can't?

What if I'm left behind?

What if I'm left in those dark misty shadows – never to return?

***

'Freddie, do you think maybe you should visit Micky?' Hettie said. 'You did say you would.'

I was with Hettie, Flo and Alice. They were walking to the factory to start work. I was simply with them to exercise my leg and to get out of the house for five minutes. Mam had been happy to see me leave with Hettie, kindly suggesting that I should 'pop into the grocers' on the way back and enquire about the job. I didn't have the energy to argue with her.

'Who is this Micky, then?' asked Flo, looking interested.

'He's that poor lad I told you about before. He was in the hospital the same time as Freddie and was badly injured.' Hettie looked over at me, her face cloaked in sympathy. 'He's got no family here – isn't that right, Fred? He must be so lonely and fed up.'

'His mam lives far away,' I said. 'And she's poorly, I think. He has no one else.'

'Oh, the poor soul.' Flo's eyes widened. 'You must visit him, Freddie. Did you know him well?'

'Pretty well. We served together.' I hesitated, really not wanting to go down this road. 'He was too injured to talk when I was in the hospital with him. I'm not even sure he'd want to see me now.'

'Oh, I'm sure he would,' Alice said in her

matter-of-fact way. 'He's probably longing for company. It must be awfully dull in there.'

I nodded slowly. 'Aye – it is that.'

'There you go,' Hettie said, nudging my arm. 'I told you, you should visit. You told the nurses you would. They said it might help his recovery to have familiar faces around.' She turned back to the girls. 'Honestly. You should have seen him. I thought our Freddie was bad, but this poor lad was bandaged head to foot.' She shuddered. 'He must be in so much pain.'

'I might go soon,' I said. 'But like I said, he might not want to see me.'

'Oh, Fred! I couldn't think why not!'

But I could. I could think of many reasons, but they were none I wanted my kid sister to know about.

The girls' chatter had now moved on to their last home match against Newcastle United Ladies at Deepdale the previous weekend. It had been a game that Martha and I had avoided because of the awful torrential rain. Mam had taken one look at the weather and told us we weren't going anywhere.

'Martha has the start of a cold,' she pointed out, gruffly. 'And I'm pretty sure that standing in the rain will do your leg no good.'

My head had been hurting pretty badly anyway, so I didn't put up much of a fight. By all accounts, the match had been a good one, but the weather had played its part.

'I've never been so wet,' Alice complained. 'I was soaked right through to my knickers.'

I turned my head away, trying to hide the blush that was already creeping up my cheeks, but it was too late, Flo had seen it.

'Aw, Freddie boy, there's no need to come over all shy.' She laughed, nudging me in the ribs. 'You should be used to seeing us with our legs out and everything.' She turned to Alice. 'You would think people wouldn't be scared of a bit of rain. Although, judging by the lack of people watching, I reckon they were worried they would melt in it.'

I scowled. 'Not all of us can stand around in that kind of weather.'

She patted my arm. 'Oh, I didn't mean you, Fred. By gum, you've been to nearly every game haven't you, with dear little Martha? I wouldn't expect you to bring her in those conditions. But where were the burly lads who reckon they can cope with everything? There only seemed to be a handful there on Saturday.'

My cheeks were still roaring. I blinked, and dipped my face away from Flo. I knew she didn't mean anything by her words, but they still stung. She obviously didn't see me as a 'burly lad'. She was like everyone else. She saw me for the weak little boy that I really was.

'It doesn't matter, anyway,' Hettie said, seemingly keen to change the conversation. I wondered if she'd noticed my discomfort. 'There was still enough money made. Mr Frankland said that we raised over one hundred and seventy-nine pounds.'

Alice breathed out. 'That's not to be sniffed at. Imagine how much better it would've been if there hadn't been a storm, though.'

'Never mind that,' Flo said. 'We have the return match to enjoy.'

'Return match?' I queried. 'Has that been confirmed, then? Are you really going up to Newcastle? It's the furthest you've been, isn't it?'

'We can't wait,' Hettie said brightly. 'I thought I had told you already, Fred? Oh, what a scatterbrain I'm becoming!'

The truth was, I had barely seen her these past few weeks. Hettie tended to work late at the factory and then stay on even later to help Mr Frankland make arrangements for the girls – writing letters and speaking to all the correct people of influence. Mr Frankland liked having her involved. He said that her calm, polite presence and excellent organisational skills made a real difference. I understood that, of course. Hettie was very important to the team. But that didn't stop me missing her.

'You must come too,' Flo said to me kindly. 'I'm sure there's room on the bus. Hettie will have a word with Mr Frankland, won't you?'

Hettie nodded keenly. 'Oh, Freddie will be coming. He has to! Mr Frankland wants him there to take the photographs.'

'Oh, good.' Flo smiled. 'And you can bring young Martha.'

I smiled. 'Oh, yes, she'll love that. If I can convince Mam ...'

Hettie nudged me. 'I'll have a word too. It's a special day. I'm sure Mam will let her.'

'Newcastle United, here we come!' roared Flo, punching the air in the glee. 'This is going to be so good, isn't it?'

'It will,' I agreed softly.

But inside, I couldn't help but be a little sad – *I* used to be the one with dreams and ambitions. I used to sit and talk to Hettie until late into the night about my dreams of travelling the world and escaping our small, dark house. Now my sisters were the ones with adventures ahead and I was no longer able to see my dreams clearly.

How had things suddenly shifted?

We reached the factory gates and I said goodbye to the girls, kissing Hettie softly on the cheek. I watched as they walked across the yard, their arms linked and their heads still bent together in chatter. I stood for a while, simply watching. They looked so jolly, so connected. I saw other girls walk over to meet them – many I recognised from the football team – Lily, Nellie, Molly. I watched as they roared with laughter in greeting. They were such a happy, united group; it was quite a sight to see.

My head heavy and my leg throbbing, I turned to make my way towards the grocers, and bumped straight into Jessie.

'Freddie! What are you doing here?'

'Jessie!' I couldn't help smiling. I found myself straightening my jacket and becoming deeply conscious of my scruffy, uncombed hair. What must she think of me?

'I walked in this morning with Hettie and the girls. I like to get regular exercise to help my leg, you know?'

I gestured at my useless limb, wishing, not for the first time, that it would miraculously get better.

'Why are you here?' I asked her. 'Don't you work in Lancaster?'

She nodded. 'I do, but I have the day off today. Mr Frankland wanted me to pop by the factory to sign some forms.' She smiled shyly. 'I think he wanted to show me around the factory too. He seems very proud of the place.'

'He is,' I agreed. 'He loves working there.'

'And where are you off to now?' she asked politely. 'Anywhere nice?'

'To the grocers,' I said reluctantly. 'I'm going to ask about the job that's going there.'

She frowned a little, it looked out of place on her features.

'Oh, it's not that bad,' I added, hurriedly. 'I'd just be glad to get a job, really. To feel useful again. It doesn't really matter what it is. I'd be lucky to get anything.'

'Really?'

I nodded firmly. 'Really.'

She touched my arm lightly. 'Well, never mind that for now, I'm just glad I saw you. I was going to speak to Hettie at the factory but I've seen you instead, which is even better.'

'Is it?' I said, my voice strangely high-pitched.

'It is. It really is.' Her eyes drifted towards the factory. 'Freddie, I'm ever so late and I know Mr Frankland is a bit of a stickler for time, but I wondered, could we meet up later? I really need to talk to you about something. Do you remember I was going to speak to my fiancé about you? Well, I did. Last night. And I need to tell you all about it.'

'Can't you explain now?' I asked, confused.

'Sorry.' She flapped her hand at me. 'There's really no time, I'm so late already. Plus, this is an excuse to have tea and cake while we talk. Wouldn't that be nice? I do love a brew!'

My cheeks immediately flared, like fire was roaring inside my mouth. 'Oh yes – that would be grand!'

She grinned. 'Is there a nice tea room near here?'

I nodded. There was indeed. In the centre of Preston. I explained whereabouts and we agreed to meet there at midday.

'And maybe,' she said, as she went to move away, 'leave going to the grocers this morning, at least 'til you've spoken further with me.'

8

'Tell me about your home.'

Johnnie nudges me as we huddle together for warmth.
It's late. I no longer care that the dirt covers every part of me,
I can barely notice the aches in my body. All I want to do is
sit here as long as possible and stare up at the dark, silky sky.
I can see a star, so distant and barely noticeable in the
swirling clouds. I wonder if perhaps my family can see it too.
If they peer up at the same sight and think of me.

'There's not much to tell,' I say. 'I live with my mam, my
dad and my two kid sisters back in Preston. It's a simple life.'

'But a good one.'

I sit back, digging my heels further into the soft ground.
'I don't know about that. I've always . . . I dunno . . .'
I hesitate suddenly, feeling conscious of my words. 'I do love
my family. Of course I do. But I've always had dreams . . .
Silly probably, but I always thought I would see the world,
do something more.' I pause. 'But perhaps I didn't expect it
to be like this.'

'I get that, lad.'

'Do you?'

'Oh yes, Freddie, I do.' In his hand, Johnnie is clutching his letter from home. He's been holding it for hours now. I expect he will sleep with it too. 'I came out here the same as you – to do something worthwhile. To fight for the cause. To prove myself.'

'I just wanted to do the right thing.'

Johnnie half laughs; it sounds hard and coarse in this cold evening light. 'And what is the right thing, eh?' He holds up the letter. 'My wife, my Betsy, she didn't want me to go to war. She writes now of how terribly afraid she is. How she misses me and wants me back. How she pines for me. But do you know the worst thing?'

'What?' I whisper.

'I'm not even sure that I want to go home.' The letter tightens in his grip. I flinch, afraid it will spoil. 'Am I the same person now? What will I do? Go back to the factory? Carry on the life I once had? After this! After everything we've seen and done.'

Far away, the gunfire rains again – it's becoming such a normal sound I barely notice it. I can't recall when I last heard a bird sing. I lower my head.

'I'm not sure I want to go back, either.' I say finally. 'I don't even know what I want to do with my life any more.'

This seems to stir Johnnie. He shifts, as if awakening from a dream and faces me directly.

'Oh, but Freddie, you are still so young. So much younger than me. You have everything in front of you.'

Johnnie takes a swig of his drink. I can smell the sharp scent of rum from here.

'You mustn't listen to me, lad,' he says, swiping his mouth. 'I'm just maudlin, thinking of home. But you – you have everything to live for.'

'If you say so.'

'Oh, I do.' His stare is piercing me, making me want to flinch. 'You, Freddie, you can go back home and do wonderful things. I know you will.'

'I don't—'

'No.' He held up his hand to silence me. 'Don't doubt yourself, lad, you need to start believing.'

The tea room was on the main high street, a small brick building set back from the rest with pretty hanging baskets outside and a large iron-framed window. We used to come here sometimes, when I was much younger. I have a memory of Mam bringing Hettie and me for a treat once, before Martha was born. She bought us a cake to share while she sat sipping tea and gazing out of the window, watching the world passing us by.

It had been so exciting, even at such a young age, to go somewhere so different and far removed from home. I remember Mam saying that Dad would have hated to have come.

'It's far too posh for your dad in here,' Mam had said, her gaze drifting around the small room, with its delicate furniture and the fine pictures hanging on the wall. 'He wouldn't feel at all comfortable.'

'You like it here though, Mammy,' Hettie said keenly. Her mouth had been full of cake and as she spoke, I could see the crumbs embedded in her teeth.

'Yes, yes I do. It reminds me of when I was a girl.' Mam had smiled weakly. 'It's such a shame we can't come here more often, isn't it?'

The question hovered between us, unanswered. I'd been suddenly overwhelmed by the sadness that I saw in my mother; I don't think I had ever seen that before. She looked like she was still longing for something, still wishing for things that hadn't come to her. I hated thinking that she felt that way. I took a bite of my half of the cake to try and distract myself, but I immediately found it difficult to chew. My mouth was so dry, and the cake seemed to be lodging in my throat in dusty lumps, making it hard to breathe. My eyes were streaming and my heart was pumping fast. I really didn't want to cough and choke up my food in this lovely tea room. That would be truly awful. Mam's watchful eyes were on me all the time; her hand began to stroke my back.

'Are you all right, Freddie?'

I nodded. 'I don't think I'm very hungry,' I'd said, pushing the cake aside. 'I'm sorry.'

Mam's eyes had widened. 'That's such a waste, Freddie.'

Waste. That was a bad word in our house. We weren't allowed to waste anything. Everything had a value, a cost. Mam would spend time adding up the price of everything she bought – working out exactly what she could afford.

And this was so much worse, of course. This was a treat that Mam had scraped together for – an extra that we never normally had.

'I'm sorry,' I muttered, lowering my head. 'I don't feel very well.'

Mam's expression had softened. 'Well – I suppose you can't help it.'

'I'll have it, Mam,' Hettie said quickly, pulling over the plate towards her own. 'I'm really hungry today.'

I glanced over at her. Hettie was a skinny little thing,

she always struggled to finish her meals at home, but the sharp look she shot me silently told me to be quiet.

Mam smiled weakly. 'Are you sure, Hettie? I don't want you to get a tummy ache.'

'It's really yummy,' Hettie replied. 'I could eat loads.'

Mam nodded. 'It used to be my favourite cake too, when I was a young girl. That's why I wanted you both to try it. I felt sad that you never had before . . .'

Me and Hettie both knew that Mam's dad, our grandfather, had been relatively well-off as families go. She had certainly lived in more comfort growing up than we had and was afforded a little more luxury.

'Do you miss it?' I'd asked her and then hesitated, suddenly feeling shy. 'I mean, do you miss your life before? Your life growing up?'

She hadn't answered straight away, her finger trailing along the rim of the delicate china cup and her gaze focused on the sights beyond the window.

'Sometimes,' she said. 'But not so often now. I don't believe in regrets. I think life puts you on a path and although you don't always understand it, you will eventually work out your proper destiny.' She'd paused, sipped her tea. 'It just might not be what you always believed it would.'

And now, here I was, back at the same tea room, years later. Instead of escaping my life, I had run back to hide in it. I shuddered. The younger me would be shocked and disappointed.

I was also pretty sure that the younger me wouldn't want to know the person I was now.

I pushed the heavy door open and was pleased to find that the bell above it still tinkled. It was such a friendly sound. The young girl behind the counter welcomed me and told me to take a seat and that she would take my order shortly. I glanced around the small room and was surprised to find Jessie already there, sitting against the far wall, sipping a cup of tea. I walked over to her. She looked up as soon as I approached.

'Freddie, dear!' She went to stand up, but I gestured that she didn't need to. 'I hope you don't mind that I ordered myself a drink already? I was so thirsty, talking away to Mr Frankland and all the girls.'

She spoke so fast it was almost overwhelming. I took a seat opposite her and carefully smoothed down my hair that I was sure had got swept up in the wind outside. I didn't want her to think of me as some scruffy boy.

Jessie giggled as I sat down. 'Oh, this is rather fun. Don't tell my sweetheart, he might get jealous.'

I smiled back nervously, the creep of a blush rising up my neck like climbing ivy. I decided to quickly change the subject. 'What did you think of the of the Dick, Kerr factory, then?'

'I thought it was a wonderful place! Similar to where I am now, I suppose, but so busy and loud. The girls that still work there seem so happy.'

'Hettie really loves working there,' I said. 'And I did too, when I was an apprentice, before the war.'

'Oh, of course, Mr Frankland mentioned that to me. I suppose you can't go back to that?'

'Mr Frankland has more than enough people working for him now,' I replied. 'And he's given girls like Hettie a job, so I can't complain really.'

Jessie smiled back politely. 'No, I don't suppose you can.'

The waitress came at that moment to take my order. I also asked for a pot of tea and politely offered to buy Jessie some cake, but she quickly declined my offer with a shake of her head. Her curls bounced prettily as she did so.

'Thanks, but no ta. I try to eat well when I'm playing. It helps my fitness and speed and makes me feel a lot better.'

'That makes sense.'

'It's hard saying no, though,' she confided. 'Especially to Victoria sponge.'

The waitress brought my tea and there was a brief silence while I poured the steaming liquid into the china cup. I wanted to try and relax. After all, this really was a treat. I looked around me at the other people sitting here. At the gentleman in the corner with his smart suit and hat, and the young woman in a pretty floral dress who was laughing loudly at his jokes.

Jessie sipped her tea and sighed loudly. Her large eyes also roamed the room.

'It's not for the likes of us, is it?' She giggled. Then she leant forward and took a deep, unladylike slurp of her tea. Her eyes were glittering with mischief. The waitress glanced over at us, looking a little put-out, but we weren't bothered. We were far too busy laughing.

'That's probably how they expect us to drink after all.' Jessie said, swiping her mouth, like my Dad did after he had downed a pint. 'I don't know why it annoys me, but it does. People making assumptions all the time.'

I nodded. I knew what she meant, of course.

'It's even more difficult when you're a girl,' Jessie continued. 'I'm still getting hassle at work from some of the lads, thinking I'm not good enough to play.

They call me names and say all kinds of nasty things.'

For the first time the sparkle in Jessie's expression had gone. She lowered her gaze.

'What do they say?' I asked quietly.

'Oh, all sorts – that I'm not really a girl at all. That I must want to be a man.' She sniffed. 'That I'm not normal. I don't understand it at all. I just like football, that's all – and I'm good at it, really good. I don't see what harm I'm doing to anybody.'

Her cheeks flushed as she talked and I noticed her scar for the first time that day. Jessie suddenly reached up and touched her cheek self-consciously.

'I hate that so much,' she said.

'You can barely see it, honestly,' I replied. 'Besides, by all accounts it was earnt through a heroic act?'

'That just makes it worse,' she said, shaking her head a little. 'The men especially seem so angry that a silly little girl like me should've done such a thing. They act like it must have been a mistake, or a fluke. They make me feel like a liar . . .'

Jessie's eyes found mine. Once again, I was taken by how warm and kind they were. I waited, not wanting to force her to talk until she was ready, Finally, her gaze dropped, and she began to speak.

'That day when the factory exploded, it was so terrifying, Freddie. I can't even tell you. The noise. The heat.' She paused, glancing up at me again. 'Sorry, you must know what that's like . . . The . . . the explosives were going off like fireworks around us – blowing up around our heads. I could smell awful, awful things. Flesh and hair burning.' She touched her own head. 'My own hair caught alight. At first, we all just ran – we wanted to get out of there as quickly as possible. But once we were outside, I looked around at the people who were there. I knew that there were people missing.' She paused again, swallowing hard. 'I could hear shouting and screaming inside the factory. What else could I do, Freddie? I couldn't leave them in there. Some people say I was a hero, but I don't think I was. I think I did what anyone else would've done in that situation. I couldn't leave people inside that burning building. So, I went back in.'

My hand froze on my cup. I licked my dry lips. 'You went back in there?'

She nodded. 'Yes. I found a group of workers, huddled together in the back of the room, so scared they could barely move. I was lucky, I suppose. I knew the factory well. I was able to guide them out quickly before the fire properly took hold.'

'How many did you save?'

She shrugged, her scar still shining red. 'I don't know – they told me after maybe ten, but I'm not certain.'

'Ten people. You saved ten people's lives.' I breathed out hard. 'Golly, Jessie, no wonder others talk of you with such high praise. You really are a hero.'

She sat back in her seat. Her expression was much cooler now. 'I don't like to be called that, Freddie, honestly I don't. It makes me uncomfortable. Like I said before, I didn't do anything that anyone else wouldn't have done. I'm nothing special. Anyone would have done the same thing. Wouldn't they?'

Her eyes demanded an answer and I found myself nodding in agreement, but of course I was being untruthful.

Because I knew for a fact that I wouldn't have been able to do it.

My tea was cooling but I drank it anyway. Jessie seemed to be studying me carefully, her expression thoughtful. Finally, after a few minutes of comfortable silence, she spoke.

'I notice you rub your head quite a bit. Does it still hurt? Has that been since the war?'

I looked down at my hands, unsure how to answer

at first, but then finally I nodded. 'Yes, I think so. I find I'm hurting all over now. Sometimes it's like I don't quite have control of my own body.'

'It's understandable, though. Your body has been put through an awful lot – the noise, the shock.' Her voice drifted a little. 'I don't think people really realise what it's like . . .'

I glanced down at my empty cup; I couldn't think of anything to say to that. Jessie's hand slid across the table and touched my own gently.

'How bad is the actual pain?' she asked softly. 'I know you've hurt your leg. Hettie told me. Does it trouble you a lot?'

'A little,' I admitted. 'But I can manage that. The limp is frustrating though. I'll never be able to run. Or play football again, which is annoying, but the pain is bearable most days.' I tapped my head. 'The pain here is worse . . . Sometimes I think my head will explode, and I still have ringing in my ears – the doctors say that will probably never go. When I notice it, it drives me mad.'

'And how do you sleep?'

I shrugged. 'I sleep when I can.'

There was a brief, drifting silence. Jessie removed her hand and rocked back on her seat. She drew another cup of tea from her pot, added the milk and then took a few careful sips. All the time her gaze was carefully fixed on me.

'I hate the night,' she said finally. 'I don't tell anyone this. I don't like to trouble them with it, but it's the time when I struggle the most. All the memories of the explosion come back to me. I dream it all over again. My mind seems to play tricks. It taunts me. It asks me if I could have done more. It sends me back into that flaming, crumbling building and makes me see things I didn't see before. Sometimes it's a child hiding in the flames, another time a young woman trapped under falling timber. My dreams make me relive the whole, horrible thing in the most awful, twisted way.'

She spoke in a gust, almost like she was desperate to get the words out of her mouth. Once she had finished, she breathed out softly and closed her eyes. I noticed how pale her skin was, how her eyes were lined with dark shadows. I wondered how often these dreams had troubled her.

'It's the same for you, isn't it?' she said, her eyes opening again. 'You have bad dreams too? I can tell by your face. You look as exhausted as I do.'

I sighed; it felt like a gentle release. 'Most nights

I have dreams where I'm back there, in the trenches. Where it feels like I'm reliving it all again. There are nights when I can't sleep at all, and some nights . . .' I shudder, my hand twitches in front of me. 'Some nights it's so twisted and cruel, it makes me too scared to ever close my eyes again.'

She nodded. 'I think it's our brain's way of dealing with the awful things we saw. I spoke to a doctor I know. He told me he hopes it will get easier in time.'

'I feel like I'm going mad,' I said, my voice cracking. 'I really do.'

'You're not, Freddie, I promise you. And you're not alone, you must remember that. You need to talk to other people. There will be so many feeling the same as you.'

I nodded slowly; my throat felt like it was closing up. I wasn't sure I could say much more.

'My younger brother was killed in 1914,' Jessie continued. Her voice was shaking a little now. She took a deep breath. 'I miss him so much. We all do. My other brothers don't talk about the war either, of what they saw, but I see how much it changed them. That's the problem with you boys, you find it hard to talk about these things.'

'It does change you,' I whispered. 'The war does that to you. It does awful, awful things.'

'There's change in this country too,' she said gently. 'And not all of it for the bad. While you boys were away fighting, it forced things to shift. Suddenly, us women were needed for more than just looking after the home. I've never really been that type of girl, so I guess for me it was kind of a relief to be allowed to actually work in a factory. To play football. I finally felt . . .' She struggled for the right word; her bright eyes found mine. 'I felt like I belonged.'

I forced back a bitter laugh. 'And yet, that's the last thing I feel. I've come home and suddenly I feel like there's no place left for me. I'm not even sure where I belong any more.'

'There is a place left for you, of course there is,' Jessie insisted. 'You need to find it, that's all. You need to find something you are good at and care about. And that's where I think I can help.'

I stared back at her, unsure. 'You can help?'

Jessie's smiled returned. It was contagious.

'I think I can, Freddie,' she said happily. 'As you know, I spoke to my fiancé about you. He has lots of friends and one of them knows the editor of the *Lancashire Daily Post*. As it happens, I met him myself briefly after that business with the explosion. He's a lovely man.'

'The *Lancashire Daily Post*?' I repeated, dumbly.

'Yes, silly, the *Lancashire Daily Post*. The editor is very keen to meet you. It seems that they might have a junior vacancy at the newspaper, and they would be interested to meet you.'

'Why would he want to meet me?'

'He knows that Mr Frankland has appointed you as our unofficial photographer and I think he was quite impressed.'

'Really?' I felt like tiny bubbles were bursting inside of my stomach. 'Jessie, this is wonderful,' I whispered. 'I don't know what to say.'

Jessie's smile looked ready to burst, too. 'You don't need to say anything. I'll come with you, if you like. I'll help where I can.'

I smiled back at her; it was impossible not to.

'Well, this is the happiest I've felt for a while,' I admitted.

And I liked the feeling very much.

I walked back home feeling somewhat lighter. Jessie had offered me a way out, a new opportunity that I was excited about for the first time since joining up to fight in the war.

As I approached our house, I heard the usual shouts and cries from Martha and the young lads she played football with. As if on cue, a ball came hurtling in my direction. If I had been in my usual shape, I would have controlled it neatly with my thigh but, as it was, I had to let it run past me.

'Hey!' Martha called out to me. 'You just missed my goal. I've already put two away past Ronnie!'

Ronnie, who looked very red-faced, smiled up at me. I was glad to see that Alfie wasn't there today. I certainly didn't want to deal with any smart comments from him.

'I was telling the lads all about the Dick, Kerr's last game and how great they were,' Martha continued. 'Ronnie says he's going to get his dad to take him to the next home match, isn't that good?'

'That is,' I said, grinning at Ronnie. 'And I've got some good news of my own, as it happens, Marth.'

'Really?' Martha looked back at me, wide-eyed.

I nodded keenly. 'I have an appointment to see the editor at the *Lancashire Daily Post* about a job, and if that goes to plan . . . well . . .' I laughed out loud. 'I will be able to tell the story of the Dick, Kerr Girls to everyone. I shall make sure the world knows about them!'

'Oh, Freddie,' Martha gasped. 'That's wonderful.'

'I haven't got the job yet,' I said, laughing, as she pulled me into a tight hug. But I couldn't help feeling a sudden rush of confidence. Everything seemed to be coming together. Surely, I could start to believe things could really improve now?

9

'She's a looker, ain't she?'

Johnny has the picture of his wife, Betsy, in front of him. It's a small, crumpled photograph of a woman with dark curls and serious-looking eyes.

'I keep her here,' he says, patting his inside pocket. 'Close to my heart.'

My heart is cold. I think I'm becoming numb to it all now. The scars of war are barely touching me. I no longer flinch when the gunfire rains overhead or when the shells explode close by.

I wonder if I will feel like this for ever.

Johnnie pushes back his hair. It's grown long these last few months. There are streaks of mud on his face and his eyes are red and sore.

'Betsy,' he repeats quietly. 'Her address is on the back of the photograph.'

'In case you forget it,' I joke.

'No,' he says, his voice serious now. 'No – in case someone needs it. In case you need it. If you need to find her, to tell her...'

I shake my head. 'No, Johnnie. I'll not listen to this now.'

'I want to know that you'll find her if anything should happen to me. I want to know that you'll tell her what happened.'

'Nothing will happen to you, Johnnie.'

'Aye.' He breathes out hard, his hand touches his chest again. 'But I'd like to know anyway. Just in case.'

I sigh. 'All right, you daft beggar. If anything should happen to you, I'll find her. I'll tell her it all.'

The promise dances from my lips; I see Johnnie's eyes light up. He claps my back and laughs.

We join the rest of the men. There is the usual jostling and joking, but I feel a dark, heavy foreboding in my stomach, like a pressing weight.

I know we are coming near our end.

The battered picture of Betsy is still buried in my top drawer, safe in my bedroom. I can't bring myself to look at it, never mind consider contacting her.

For what would I tell her if I did?

What would she think of me if she knew the truth?

I stopped outside the large, imposing three-storey building that stood at 127 Fishergate and housed the

Lancashire Daily Post. It was heavily decorated with grand arch openings and topped with an impressive flagpole. I hovered briefly at the door, my muscles tightening under my best suit and my mouth suddenly dry. Instinctively, I licked my lips.

'The editor is dead friendly,' Jessie said, beside me. 'Seriously, Freddie, what do you have to lose?'

I shrugged. 'Not much, I suppose.'

'Well, then.' She paused, looking me carefully up and down. 'Would you like me to come in with you? Be a bit of moral support?'

'Would you mind?' I replied, feeling a bit daft. 'I think I'd like that.'

Jessie immediately giggled. 'Of course I don't, you daft apeth. That's why I offered. It would be my pleasure.'

'Thank you!'

She offered her arm to me and winked cheekily. 'Come on then, let's get this show on the road.'

The office itself was bright and lively, full of loud chatter and non-stop clatter from the large typewriters on many of the desks. At one end was a group of women, sitting closely together and gossiping loudly as they typed. Their eyes cast over us as we passed them by. Then one of the women, a tall blonde with rather large nose, shrieked in sudden recognition.

'Jessie! It's Jessie Walmsley, isn't it?'

Jessie turned towards the woman, her smile still bright and engaging, but her expression a little confused. 'Yes, I am. Hello. Do I know you?'

The woman giggled. 'Oh no, lass, I'm afraid not. But I know you! I've been following the Dick, Kerr Girls and I know you've just started for them.'

Jessie's smile immediately intensified. 'Oh, it's so lovely to meet a fan.'

'I keep telling the girls to go and watch,' the woman gestured at her colleagues. 'But they don't listen.'

One, a cheerful-looking dark-haired girl, looked over in her direction. 'I keep telling you, Rita, I'm not interested in sport.'

Rita shrugged. 'More's the pity, you're missing out on a right treat.' She turned her attention back to Jessie. 'Are you here for an interview?'

'Well, we are, but not for me,' Jessie replied. 'My friend Freddie here has a meeting with the editor.'

'Oh.' Rita looked me up and down, her tongue probing her cheek. 'You're quite a young one, aren't you?'

'I'm seventeen,' I replied stiffly, attempting to stand taller.

'And a war hero,' Jessie added unnecessarily. 'Is the editor's office at the end?'

'Oh, aye.' Rita sounded bored now. 'It's right at the back, you can't miss it.' She quickly whipped off the sheet of paper from the typewriter. 'His name's Mr Jackson. He's not a bad sort. Just watch your P's and Q's.'

'Thank you,' I said.

We walked quickly through the rest of the office, past a pool of young men sitting at their desks – some on the phone and others scribbling on their notepads. At the last desk we passed a large, jolly-looking man with flushed cheeks. I noticed he had the newspaper open at the sports section. He looked up.

'All right? Are you here for me?'

'We're here for Mr Jackson,' Jessie replied, gesturing at the glass office behind his desk. On the door was the word 'editor'.

'Ah, right,' the man said grinning. 'You're here for the lackey job, eh?'

'Lackey?' I blinked back at him.

'Yeah, lackey. The one we get to do the jobs we don't want to do.' He laughed loudly, one hand smoothing down his greasy hair. 'Good luck, boy. That's all I can say.'

'Ignore him, Freddie,' Jessie hissed.

But as I slowly rapped on the glass door, I couldn't ignore the sinking feeling inside of me.

'Ignore Gordon,' Mr Jackson said as we walked into his small, cosy office. He gestured towards the two chairs opposite his desk and we sat ourselves down. 'I heard what he said to you. Our esteemed sports reporter likes to tease, that's all. I only put up with his foolish ways because he's a damn good reporter. Now then, I take it you must be Freddie?'

'Yes, sir.'

'Well, it's grand to meet you, lad,' Mr Jackson replied, shaking my hand. He then turned briefly to Jessie. 'Ey up, Jessie love. How are you?'

'Oh, I'm good, ta,' she replied sweetly. 'But it's not me you're wanting to see.'

Jessie touched my shoulder. 'I'll wait outside, Freddie.' She flashed me a bright smile, it felt like a good luck signal.

Mr Jackson waited until Jessie had left the room and then clamped his hands on the desk and stared hard at me. 'So tell me, Freddie. Why would you like to work for a newspaper?'

I swallowed, fighting back the sick feeling that was

rising up inside me. I carefully placed my hands on my lap, hoping Mr Jackson wouldn't notice them shaking with nerves.

I stared back at Mr Jackson and attempted to compose myself. He was a smallish man, with a balding head and bright blue eyes that seemed to have many questions behind them.

'I think I have lots to offer, sir,' I said finally. 'I'm young, quick to learn and keen to do well.'

He nodded. 'And you have an interest in news reporting? This is what I was led to believe by Jessie's young man.'

'Sports reporting in particular,' I said carefully. 'I'm already taking photographs of the Dick, Kerr Girls and I think I have a pretty good knowledge of the game. If there was a vacancy in this area . . .'

Mr Jackson sat back quickly. 'Sadly, there isn't. As I said, Gordon is our sports reporter, and I have a very good sports photographer too, Simon Smith. Simon has mentioned moving to London, mind . . .'

'Really?' I shifted in my seat. 'Maybe I could replace him?'

'No,' Mr Jackson said sadly. 'No, that's not an option. Simon has a junior working with him. Bobbie Saunders.

Bobbie would take over.'

'Is there any work I could do on the sports desk?' I asked hopefully.

Mr Jackson sighed gently. 'I wish I had something there, lad. I would love to help you out. You know I lost my own lad in the war. He was your age too. Died at Ypres.'

'I was at Ypres,' I whispered. 'It was my last battle.'

'His too,' Mr Jackson said sadly. He rubbed his chin, studying me carefully. 'It's daft, but I almost feel like Reggie himself sent you to me. It makes me feel like I need to do right by you.'

'I would be so grateful, sir, and I promise to work hard.'

'I don't doubt that. Now, all I have at the moment is a vacancy on the 'wanted' desk. It's very junior, typing up the classified advertisements, but it's a step on the rung, so to speak.'

I considered it for a moment. It wasn't sports reporting, but it could be a good opportunity. Surely a foot in the door was better than a closed door?

I nodded. 'I'll take it.'

Mr Jackson smiled. 'It's not the most glamorous job, but it will keep you out of trouble. In the meantime, you're welcome to keep me posted on the work you are doing for Mr Frankland and the team.'

'I can show you my photographs?' I offered.

'Indeed,' he replied. 'You never know. If you get a good one, it could change things.'

10

I'm back in the sludge, now deep in the trenches.

I can't remember when I was last properly dry. My feet are riddled with sores and festering wounds, my uniform is constantly damp and heavy against my skin. I don't think I will ever be warm again. A kind of cold, dampness has sunk right into my bones; it has settled right into the marrow. We don't even shiver any more; our teeth barely chatter, it's like our bodies have adjusted to this feeling, a kind of rotting from the inside out.

We smell of rot too, each of us. It is curdling in my throat. It's making me want to choke.

Johnnie is stood next to me. He's keeping watch. We take it in turns. Some wait, guns pressed over the edge, ready to take action should it be required, and others rest – if rest is possible. We close our eyes for the briefest of moments. Sleep comes in short, cruel drifts, even as we stand, our bodies stumbling in the small, tight space. Sometimes it's best not to close your eyes at all. This is what Johnnie says. Johnnie thinks it's better to stay alert.

'We need to be prepared at all times,' he says, his voice rich and loud over the sound of distant gunfire. 'When the time comes, we need to be ready. I'll not have the blighters catch us out.'

He tugs on my arm. He makes me stand upright.

'Keep your head together, Freddie. The time will come when I'll need you. I'll need you to help me.' He faces me. In the poor light I can see the flash of his bright teeth, the slight twinkle in his eyes. 'You can't let a brother down, can you?'

'No,' I say back, my voice weaker. 'No, I won't.'

'This nonsense will soon be over. You'll soon be back home, where was it again? Preston?' I nod slowly in reply, tears biting at my eyes. 'You'll soon be home lad, back in the arms of your family. And they'll be so pleased. They'll hug their hero son, won't they? They'll be proud of you and everything you've done.'

'But I've not done anything,' I say back.

'Not yet. But your chance will come . . .'

To the right of us there is an explosion, bright sparks light up the night. Johnnie swears under his breath and suddenly all I can hear is gunfire raining in all directions.

'So, it begins,' he hisses.

***

I had a little desk at the *Lancashire Daily Post*, quite near the back of the busy office but close enough to the secretaries that I could occasionally listen in to their laughter and banter. I liked it there. Despite the fact it was loud and busy, I found I could easily lose myself in the atmosphere. The noise was more constant and didn't trouble me as much. Everyone who worked here was keen to make the newspaper as successful as possible and, after the war, a flood of good news stories was overtaking the rest. As the days flew by, I found myself settling in quite nicely.

I was also quite near to Gordon, the burly sports reporter who had teased me on the day of my interview. His attitude towards me hadn't much changed and although he was friendly enough, he spent most of the day ordering me to make him tea.

'Never mind, son,' he said, after I gave him his fifth cup for that particular day. 'When you've been a reporter for as long as I have, you'll get to boss the new lad about.'

I kept quiet, not wanting to say that if I was a reporter, I wouldn't treat the 'new lad' in that way. I liked to think I'd be much more helpful, and kinder.

But it wasn't all bad. At least by coming over to Gordon's desk, I was pulled away from my own work, which I wasn't enjoying as much as I'd hoped. The 'wanted' advertisements were a little dull and the customers that placed them could be quite grumpy and impatient. I was also struggling to type them out on the rickety typewriter. The girls kept looking over and laughing at how slow I was. Rita joked that her two-year-old boy would be faster. But Gordon's work . . . well, that was far more interesting!

'Is that the Blackburn game?' I said, peering over his arm.

'Aye.' Gordon was reading through the copy, his eyes screwed up in concentration. 'It was a tough one.'

I leant in a little, noticing a tiny section in the corner of the page. 'And is that a piece on the Dick, Kerr Girls?' I asked.

'Yes, why?'

'It's . . . well, it's very small . . .' I said cautiously.

Gordon frowned. 'It's fine as it is. It's a girls' football team. We don't need to make a big fuss about it.'

'But . . .'

He turned to me, a sly smile curling on his face. 'Freddie, I know you're keen on the team. I know you're chums with them or whatever, but you really do know nothing about reporting. Now, why don't you skip along back to your little "wanted" desk and leave me to get on with the real work.'

The day only got worse. Just as I was about to leave, Mr Jackson called me to his office.

'Freddie,' he said, rather sternly. 'Take a seat.'

I saw that he was clutching the latest edition of the newspaper. It was open at the 'wanted' section and an advertisement was circled several times in dark pen. Noticing that I was looking, he jabbed the page several times.

'Do you know what you've done?'

'No, sir,' I replied, flustered.

He pushed the newspaper towards me. I recognised the advertisement immediately – how could I forget? The woman who had placed it with us had been the most rude and uptight person I'd met in quite some time and had barked her instructions at me as if I were some kind of idiot. I read the piece again, painfully remembering how long it had taken for me to type up.

Wanted – respectable young girl for light housework and chores.
References required. Contact the housekeeper, Mrs Evans, at Westbury Farm

'I don't understand what I did wrong, sir,' I said finally, after reading the advertisement twice over. There were no typing mistakes that I could see.

'You don't understand?' Mr Jackson prodded the paper again. 'You completely messed it up. Mrs *Westbury* is the housekeeper at *Evans* Farm. Mrs Evans, the lady of the house, was not pleased to receive calls referring to her as the housekeeper. She came in herself to complain. You were fortunate to be on your lunchbreak at the time, or she would have burnt your ear off too. I spent half an hour listening to her mithering on!'

I slapped my forehead. 'Of course, Mrs Westbury is the housekeeper! How could I forget her!' After all, she was the awful, bossy woman that came in. She must have that in common with her employer! 'I'm so sorry, sir. I got into such a muddle with the typewriter. And Mrs Westbury got me in a bit of a state with her demands – my notes were rushed and I couldn't make head or tail of them. I'll take better care next time.'

'You need to do better, Freddie lad. Mrs Evans is an important landowner and has a lot of influence around here. We can't be upsetting locals.'

'I'm sorry, sir.'

Mr Jackson sighed slowly. 'That's all right, lad.

You'll learn, I hope.' He hesitated; his eyes fixed on mine. 'Just don't make me regret my decision in hiring you, will you now?'

'No, sir,' I replied quietly, my heart beating fast. 'I will make this up to you. I promise.'

And I quickly left the room.

Back at home, Hettie was full of excited gossip about the new girls that were to be joining the team. Martha and I sat and listened to her in the front room while Mam prepared dinner. It was nice to hear her being so merry. By all accounts, there were two new Alices – Alice Woods and Alice Norris – but there was also another young lass who might be starting soon. Lily Parr. Hettie seemed particularly excited about her.

'Mr Frankland is making plans to talk to Lily soon,' Hettie said. 'She's only young. Fourteen, I believe, but Mr Frankland thinks she's the bee's knees.'

Martha's eyes immediately grew rounder. 'Fourteen? That's only a few years older than me.'

'Aye, Martha.' Hettie affectionately draped an arm around Martha's shoulders. 'I told you it won't be long. If you keep at it, you might be able to train with the girls soon.'

'That would be wonderful,' Martha breathed.

'Fourteen is the same age as your other new girl too, isn't it?' I asked. 'Now, is that Alice Norris or Alice Woods?'

I was becoming very confused as so many of the girls shared the same name. It was hurting my head a little.

Hettie laughed at my pained expression. 'Alice *Norris* has just started at the factory and yes, she is fourteen too. Alice Woods is joining us from Liverpool Ladies and is older. But both girls are lovely and will fit into the team really well.' She paused. 'Did I tell you that it was Alice Woods that recommended Lily Parr to Mr Frankland?'

'No,' I said.

'Oh, well, she did. She told Mr Frankland she believed we could be the best football team in the country, but that we'd be even better if Lily Parr was playing. And when Mr Frankland asked her who this Lily Parr was, Alice told him that Lily was playing for St Helens – a team Alice had faced herself in charity fundraising events in Merseyside. Alice said that this Lily stood out from everyone else and blew the crowd away. She knew then that she wanted to play football on the same side as Lily.'

'And I bet Mr Frankland agreed to that straight away.'

'Oh, indeed. I think he went to watch a few matches

himself. Now all he talks about is Lily Parr. Lily Parr and the two new Alices. "The fantastic threesome" that will strengthen our side.'

I smiled wanly. 'Well, it certainly seems as if things are coming together for you. At least you had a good day.'

Hettie scowled a little. 'You don't seem yourself, Freddie. Is something wrong?'

'Not really.' I rubbed at my head, wishing the muzzy feeling would disappear. 'I made a daft mistake, that's all, but the editor is bound to think I'm nowt but a useless boy now. He'll never consider me for any other work.'

'It's still early days, though . . .'

'Aye, but I need to impress him and all I keep doing is messing up.'

Martha leant over and squeezed my knee. 'Don't worry yourself, Fred. He'll soon see how hardworking you are.'

'Yes, Marth is right,' Hettie said. 'And you will impress, just you wait. All you need is the right opportunity.'

'And what opportunity will that be?' I asked. 'Gordon will never let me help him.'

Hettie paused. 'I'm not supposed to say anything yet, but there might be something big happening soon – something that you can take photographs of before anyone else . . . it could be a bit of a scoop – for you, and for the *Lancashire Daily Post.* '

'What is it?' I asked, intrigued. 'What's happening?'

'Well . . . the French Ladies team are coming to England to play our girls!' Hettie said. 'It's being arranged right now. It's still very hush, hush but I can trust both of you, can't I?'

'Aye,' Martha and I both breathed.

'A French tour will attract lots of attention,' Hettie continued, her face glowing. 'And you, Freddie, you can be right in the centre of it.'

11

I was so tired that night. So very tired.
   I knew I needed to step up, to take my place.
   But I couldn't do it.
   God forgive me, but I couldn't do it.

I woke early to find Hettie sitting on the end of my bed. I realised the heaviness of her body by my feet must have disturbed me. The light was still weak in the room, spilling through the small dusty window. Outside, I could hear the milk cart making its way slowly up the road. Someone, further away, was whistling. In the next bed, Martha, still asleep, was snoring gently. Another day was beginning. I rubbed at my eyes and pulled myself up a little, my body stiff and awkward.

'You were calling out another name in your sleep,' Hettie said, leaning towards me. Her hair was sticking up all over the place. She yawned loudly and stretched, tipping her head back. 'You kept saying it over and over – this time it was Micky Adams. The lad from the hospital.'

'Sorry,' I muttered, rubbing my eyes. 'Did I wake you?'

'Well, yes you did, but that doesn't matter. I had to get up early, anyway.' She glanced over at Martha, who was laid on her back with her mouth wide open, ready to catch flies. 'I don't know how she can sleep through it, though. I swear our kid would still be snoring away if a herd of elephants trampled through the room.'

I chuckled, despite myself. 'She has no worries, that lass. She sleeps like an angel.'

Hettie tugged at the fringe of my bed cover. I watched as her fingers twisted the tassel round and round. Finally, she spoke again.

'Micky Adams . . . He's the lad I told you to visit. I remember his head was all bandaged up when you were in hospital together. The nurse told me he got the mustard gas bad.'

I nodded. 'Aye, he did.'

'He wouldn't talk, would he?' She hesitated. 'Did he ever talk to you?'

I pulled myself up further in the bed. My insides had turned to jelly. What should I tell her? That I wanted to talk to Micky, I really did, but every time I'd moved towards his bed, my throat had constricted, my tongue had snapped back in my mouth. How could

I speak to him? He had been there in the final moments. He had been there with me and Johnnie. He knew what had happened.

'He didn't talk at all,' I replied softly.

At least, I'd never given him the opportunity to.

'The poor lad.' She paused. 'Like I said, you really should see him again. Try again. Maybe he'd speak this time.'

'Maybe,' I said. 'I dunno, Hettie. Some things are best left—'

'But you called his name. It's like before, when you called out for that other lad. That Johnnie. You always sound so upset . . . so . . . well, frightened. It scares me.'

I smiled weakly at her. 'You have no reason to be scared, Hettie.'

She frowned a little and rubbed at her mouth. 'You are getting better, aren't you, Freddie? Please say you are?' She paused. 'You are happy, aren't you?'

'I'm very happy,' I said.

But the lie felt as hollow as my stomach, once I said it.

The weeks passed quickly, and I was kept quite busy at the newspaper. I was still struggling to type out the advertisements, but luckily, I had been given much easier customers and the typewriter was becoming slightly easier to use with time. I was lucky too that the secretaries felt sorry for me and often helped me if I ran into bother. Rita especially had taken me under her wing.

'How can we resist helping?' she would say, smiling. 'Besides, you make a decent brew and you're polite, unlike some . . .'

I watched as her scornful glare landed on Gordon. Not that he would care. Gordon didn't seem to mind what anyone else thought.

As we were approaching spring, the weather was warming up and sunlight was flooding into the office, which also helped to lift my mood. It was true that I found the long, dark days of winter harder. It reminded me too much of the cold nights on the Front. Sunshine and blue sky always seemed more hopeful, it offered a fresh start and it even gave me a slight bounce in my otherwise wonky step.

Besides, I had reasons to be happier other than the weather. Exciting things were happening for the Dick, Kerr Ladies team and it was impossible not to be swept up in the melee of it all, especially with Hettie telling us about it at home. The French international games had finally been confirmed earlier this month and the

French Ladies team was due to arrive at Preston later that day to start their ten-day tour, kicking off with a game against the Dick, Kerr Girls at Deepdale. The Dick, Kerr Girls would then play the French Ladies in games across the country. Hettie had been beside herself this morning. This was the beginning of the team playing international matches – they really had taken the next big step.

'You can take photographs of their arrival, Freddie,' she said excitedly. 'If you get a decent one, Mr Jackson has to notice, surely?'

I couldn't help but grin back. 'It's worth a try, isn't it?'

Gordon had obviously noticed my happier mood in the office. He came over to my desk and nudged me gently.

'You seem to be in a grand mood today.'

'Am I?' I said back. 'It must be the weather.'

'Perhaps.' Gordon eyed me cautiously and then gestured to the secretary pool. 'I heard you talking to the girls this morning. Something about a French team coming over?'

'Oh, you didn't know?' I tried to look surprised. Of course, in truth I wasn't. Gordon had no interest in women's football. 'One of the best French women's teams are coming here to play the Dick, Kerr Girls. Part of a tour.'

'Really? Interesting. So, these French women – do you reckon they're any good?'

I shrugged. 'I'm not sure, but I'm sure they will give the Dick, Kerr Girls some tricky games.'

Gordon nodded, his mouth busy chewing on the end of a pen. 'And where else are the French girls playing us on this tour?'

'Here first, and then Stockport, Manchester and Chelsea,' I replied. 'Mr Frankland already went down to Dover to meet them and accompany them to London. He wanted them to feel truly welcome and comfortable in our country. Our girls are so excited to be playing, too. Mr Frankland thinks it will be an excellent opportunity for them.'

'Quite a tour, then.'

'Are you interested in covering it?' I asked.

Gordon screwed up his face. 'Some short pieces, I expect. I have proper sports events to cover, after all. No one is really that interested, though, are they?'

'I'm not sure that's true,' I replied carefully. 'There's already a lot of talk in Preston about it. People seem to be getting quite excited about the first game. I imagine there will be a good crowd on the day.'

Gordon nodded slowly. 'Well, maybe I'll pop along

for a bit. I should get Simon or Bobbie to take some photographs . . .'

'I could do that,' I suggested. 'I mean, I will be there anyway, taking photographs for Mr Frankland. Perhaps I could take some for you, too?'

Gordon merely laughed. 'Thanks lad, but that's not necessary. Leave the proper job to us men, eh?'

And then, still chortling to himself, he walked back to his cluttered and messy desk.

It was difficult to describe the wonderful atmosphere as we waited for the French Ladies to arrive at the train station. The crowds really were quite immense. I suppose it was akin to the end-of-war celebrations, except that day had been edged with sadness – a remembrance that so many had been hurt or killed, and a longing that nothing similar should happen again. These celebrations were quite different. People were excited and joyful. They were expectant and cheeky. It was almost as if the king himself had chosen to walk our streets and visit our homes. I think we felt special for once.

Beside me, Martha pulled on my coat. Having got here early, we were stood right at the front of the platform. I knew this was my chance to take some great photographs. I only hoped I could get one good enough to show Mr Jackson what I was capable of.

'When will the train arrive? Will it be soon?'

Martha and I had come alone, Martha knowing that she had to be patient while I took my pictures. Hettie was in another part of the crowd with some of the football girls who were keen to welcome their opposition.

'It should be—'

Just as I spoke, the train whistled its approach, drawing slowly into platform like a triumphant beast. The crowd immediately roared with pleasure and the Dick, Kerr brass band, who had been standing just behind us, immediately started playing the Marseillaise – the French national anthem. It really was a perfect arrival.

Martha immediately squealed and jumped up and down so that she could see. 'They're here! The French girls are here! Do you think they are quite beautiful and elegant? I bet they are.' She breathed out hard. 'Oh, look, Freddie. I can see them. They are coming out. Oh . . .'

I positioned my camera, ready to take the perfect shot.

The French team began to step off the train, cheering and waving back at the crowd. They were all dressed in neat coats and pretty little hats, and each face that looked towards us was lit up with smiles. They really were a merry band of women.

One of the taller girls whooped loudly and waved what looked like a scruffy toy rabbit in the air.

'Oh, look,' Martha said, pointing. 'I bet that's her lucky mascot. How wonderful it is that she brought it along with her.'

The crowd began to press forward and it was difficult to keep my place, but I pressed my body into the surge, holding firm.

'Hold on to my coat, Martha,' I ordered. 'I don't want to lose you in the crowd.'

I managed to keep my spot, in front of many other press photographers who'd arrived after us. The tall French girl turned to face me, waving her mascot high in the air. I quickly took my shot, her face lighting up as the camera bulbs popped.

I knew it was a good one. I could feel it in my bones.

Hettie had told me that the girls had a mixture of backgrounds. These women were dressmakers, typists, bookkeepers and shop assistants. Hard-working, skilled women who also loved to play football.

'I can't remember such excitement over a football team for a long time,' a man next to me mused.

'And for a group of women too. Who would've thought it, eh? The world really is turning on its axis.'

Looking at the happy crowds around me I couldn't help but agree.

'But maybe the world needed to turn,' I replied. 'Maybe this has been a long time coming.'

After the photographs were finished, I moved myself and Martha through the crowd so that we could watch more easily. Hettie and some of the more experienced players were being introduced to the French Ladies by Mr Frankland. I couldn't help but feel proud of my kid sister. Hettie would be so pleased to meet another great female football team, and especially one from overseas.

'Hettie is so lucky,' Martha breathed.

'She certainly won't forget this day in a hurry,' I replied, smiling.

A bouquet of flowers was presented to a very grand-looking woman clothed in a heavy coat, her dark hair was swept into a neat chignon at the back of her head. I realised it must be Madame Millat, the manager of the French team. She accepted the flowers warmly and hugged them to her body. It was clear that both she and her team were moved by the welcome they had received here. Our two countries had been so scarred by war. My stomach swirled again with the importance of this moment.

'Look, Marth – most of the French girls are all quite small, like you. I bet they're nippy down the wing,' I said. 'Hettie told me their manager really is very experienced and has a background in association football in France. I know she thinks our girls could learn so much from a woman like that.'

A lady who was standing just in front of us turned round. Her face glowed as she grinned at both of us. It was only as she spoke, and the lilt of her accent was revealed, that I realised she was with the team.

'Madame Millat – who you speak of – is a most marvellous woman,' she said, her dark eyes studying us carefully. 'You should remember what Madame said once, little one, for it's very important. It has stayed with me for a long, long time.'

'What was it?' asked Martha, unable to contain her excitement.

The woman smiled. 'She said this: "In my opinion, football is not wrong for women. I do not think it is unwomanly to play football as they do not play like men, they play fast but not vigorous football".'

'So, she thinks the men still play better?' Martha asked, looking confused.

'No, no chérie. You misunderstand.' The lady paused, considering her words before speaking again. 'She means the women play a different game, a beautiful game. A game of their own. There is no need for comparisons, no need to exclude us.' She laid her hand on Martha's shoulder. 'We can do it our way.'

12

Misty, thick air is whipping around us. It's so cold in this trench. Oh God, have I ever felt this cold before? I'm shivering, but the chills seem to be coming right from the core of my body. I'm struggling to keep still.

Micky is bellowing for us to take position. The gunfire is loud, so loud. I actually think that my ears will explode with the pressure.

'I can't do this,' I sob. 'I just want to sleep. I can't stand up.'

I'm so tired. I've never known anything like this before. My entire body aches. I just want to slump to the floor. My legs are jelly. I cannot do it.

'Johnnie,' I call weakly.

Johnnie turns to me; his face is twisted in anguish. He needs me beside him. I know this. He's tired too. But I can't do it. I can't move.

Meanwhile, Micky is bellowing at both of us. He needs help. We are under fire. We are in danger. We need to attack.

'I can't,' I say again. My body sinks further towards the ground.

'It's all right,' Johnnie says, a gentle smile glinting on his tired face. 'Stay there.'

I watch, speechless, as he turns and climbs back against the embankment, shifting over a little so he covers the spot where I should have stood. His gun rests on the edge, his body is stiff and primed.

I watch and my entire body slumps to the floor. I think I may never get up again.

As the guns explode around us, I don't think any more. I forget all about promises and debts owed. I forget all about friendship and brotherhood. I forget it all.

I just close my eyes.

Mr Jackson peered down at the photographs I took of the French team. In particular, the one I took of the girl I later discovered was their captain, waving her mascot. Behind him, his large ornate clock ticked loudly and his open window let through the sounds from outside – a passing van, a crying baby, the roar of market sellers. After what seemed like an eternity, he finally spoke.

'I like this one. It's very good,' he said. 'You've really captured something here, lad.'

'It was really thrilling being there, sir. All the business and chatter. I was dead lucky to get that shot, I think.'

'It's more than luck,' he replied, studying the other pictures. 'You seem to have an eye for this. All of these photographs are very good. Not only are they well taken, but you've captured – I don't know – a certain energy.'

I felt my cheeks redden. 'Thank you, sir.'

'Not at all. I'm impressed, lad.' He looked up, his eyes warm. 'I asked you to impress me and you did. I can see now why Mr Frankland has been so keen for you to help him.'

'He's been helping me too, sir. He develops all my photographs for me. These included.' I paused, and then carefully handed him another picture. 'This was the team shot I took of the Dick, Kerr Girls most recently. Mr Frankland thinks it's one of my best.'

Mr Jackson took it from me and spent a moment or two carefully looking at it.

'They are quite a team, aren't they?' he said finally. 'You can see their strength here. Their determination. It's a very clear photograph.'

'Thank you,' I said again.

'I can see why you want to be a photographer.' Mr Jackson placed the photograph back down on the desk. His fingers stroked the edges. 'You know a lot about the Dick, Kerr Girls, don't you?'

I nod. 'Ever such a lot. My sister Hettie is involved with the team too, so it's all we talk about at home.'

'Indeed.' He pushed the photo back towards me. 'Now. You may not have heard, but Simon is sadly leaving us. Bobbie, by all accounts, should take over, but . . . Well, let's just say his skills leave something to be desired.'

My hopes soared. 'Do you mean . . . could I . . . ?'

He sat back, folding his arms across his chest. 'We could trial you, lad. How about that? You can cover the French tour here for me. Gordon will be busy elsewhere and I do believe these games need a little more attention.'

'Does that mean you want me to write up the matches, too?'

'Just short pieces.' He smiled. 'Normally I'd have two people from the paper attend, but these are still small games . . .'

I stepped forward and shook his hand eagerly.

'You won't regret this, sir,' I said.

'No,' he replied dryly. 'I hope I won't. Now, you'd better hurry on. I believe you have your first match to cover tonight.'

'I have,' I replied, grinning.

And I couldn't wait to begin.

***

A poster was pinned on the fence outside the ground.

LEST WE FORGET – the French ladies are playing here, for the lads who played the game over there!

I couldn't help but read the poster a few times. I could feel an uneasiness building inside of me. I had been one of those that had been 'over there'. As much as I was excited for the game, I half-wished that it wasn't still connected with the war. I wanted to break all my memories of war for ever – just cut the ties and move on.

After all, it had been a poster like this that had enticed me into going in the first place. I could still see it now, stuck up outside the town hall. 'Your country needs you' it had told me in large black letters – and I had believed it. I had actually thought that I could make a difference by going to war. I'd thought it might give me some purpose.

How daft I had been.

'Are you all right, Freddie?' Hettie asked.

'Yes, hurry up, Freddie,' Martha muttered impatiently. She had come too, of course. How could we keep her away from this game? 'It's just a silly poster. Why are you frowning at it like that?'

'It's nothing,' I said, shaking my head slowly. 'Nothing at all. You're right, let's hurry. We don't want to miss the start.'

And I was better off pushing these silly thoughts away to where they belonged. At the back of my mind.

We sat pitch-side – a camera in my hands, a notepad on my lap and an excited Martha beside me. Both of us were wrapped in heavy coats, on Mam's insistence, for, despite it being a spring night, there was still a chill in the air.

Dad had even questioned Hettie a little about the French team before we left. Apparently, a lot of his friends down the pub had been discussing the upcoming match and were very impressed that our girls should encourage international interest. He seemed quite excited by it all. I'd suggested that Dad come with us to the game, but he shrugged off the idea, claiming 'his back hurt too much'. I couldn't help noticing the sad look of longing that passed across his face as we left the house. I wondered how much he would've liked to have joined us if he had been in less pain. It was so sad.

And yet all those thoughts were gone now that I was back here at the Deepdale ground. Once again, the atmosphere was electrifying. The crowd, already in good form, were singing and cheering at the tops of their voices, alongside the Dick, Kerr band, which was playing loudly.

'The French Ladies must be impressed by this,' I said to Martha. 'We really have gone to town.'

Martha nodded. 'I can't wait to see them play. I think it will be close.' She leant forward, obviously looking for a glimpse of one of her favourite players. 'I hope Jessie plays tonight – and Alice Woods. I really want to see them.'

'I think they will,' I said, scribbling some introductory notes on my pad.

The Dick, Kerr band suddenly stopped. We all looked up as a brief hush fell upon the crowd. Martha nudged me in the ribs.

'Look – this is it. They're coming out.'

Both teams were running out on to the pitch – and they really did look grand. The French girls wearing their smart light-blue jerseys and navy-blue shorts and our very own Dick, Kerr Girls dressed in their usual black-and-white stripes, complemented by their neatly fitted striped caps.

'Oh . . .' said Martha. 'I feel quite nervous now.'

The band struck up a tune again and the crowd roared with anticipation. As the teams lined up neatly, the band played each national anthem in turn. First the *Marseillaise* and then *Rule Britannia* – which the crowd sung along to with glee. I could feel my skin prickle and my heart beat a little faster. It was almost as if I was out there on the pitch myself, ready to face battle.

I looked around at the sheer volume of the crowds.

'They reckon there's at least 25,000 here today,' the journalist next to me stated. I didn't recognise him and assumed from his heavy Scouse accent that he worked for a newspaper in Liverpool.

I nodded my thanks to him and scribbled the number on my pad. 25,000. That really was quite a number. Mr Jackson would be impressed by that, surely!

We watched as Mr Conner, the general manager of the Dick, Kerr factory – and as Hettie had previously told us, a rather nice gentleman – began the game by kicking off. It was quite a sight to see this suited chap walk confidently on to the pitch to take the shot. I wondered privately what the girls must have thought of his rather stunted kick, but it didn't seem to matter. The crowd loved it and roared with excitement and Mr Conner, obviously swept up in the emotion of the day, threw his arms up to the sky and beamed, as though he had just scored the winning goal.

This was it. The whistle promptly blew. The game had begun.

It was immediately fast and fraught. I found I could barely dare to take my eye off the ball to write in my notepad, in case I missed the action.

Our girls started extremely well, moving the ball across the pitch quickly. For a while it was almost as if they had brought the French defence to a standstill. They seemed to be frozen in position, looking around at each other, shocked at how effectively the Dick, Kerr Girls were moving past them.

It wasn't long before our winger, Lily Lee, released a ball to Jennie Harris, who was in plenty of space. She looked up and lofted it beautifully to Flo Redford, who was on the edge of the penalty area. Flo controlled the ball on her chest and then struck it on the half-volley into the back of the net.

1–0.

The noise from the crowd was unprecedented. Next to me, Martha was jumping up and punching the air with her fists.

'Flo! Is there anyone better?'

The action didn't stop there. The French, clearly shaken by the goal, were now driven into action. They used their speed to drive forward and attempted to pierce through the Dick, Kerr defence. But Jessie and Alice Kell were rock solid in their positions and quickly broke up the threat of attack.

'Isn't Jessie strong?' Martha said keenly. 'She always seems to keep a clear head.'

'She certainly does,' I replied as I scrawled down more notes, my eyes still fixed on the game. It was impossible to tear myself away; I was terrified that I might miss something.

Time was ticking towards the half-time whistle and the Dick, Kerr Girls were once again dominating possession. Despite the French goalkeeper being extremely skilled, drawing applause from the crowd when she saved a drilling volley by Flo, our girls tore through the French defence and made at least three or four attacks on goal. One, by Jennie Harris, was particularly impressive – she dribbled past two French defenders, although unfortunately she then drove the ball against the post.

But then, moments before the whistle was due to be blown, Lily Lee, our sharp and very fast winger, was brought down by a nasty tackle. I saw the flash of pain on her face as she fell to the ground, her hand clasping her boot.

'Oh no!' gasped Martha. 'I hope she's not badly hurt.'

'Me too,' I replied grimly. Lily had been instrumental on the left flank, driving the ball forward and unsettling the French defence. We were only one goal ahead. We couldn't afford to lose her.

I picked up my camera and took a picture of Lily being carried off the field by two first aid workers. Her face looked pained but determined. I knew that she would be frustrated to be coming off the pitch so soon.

I read back through my notes during half-time – there would surely be enough in there already to write a decent enough report for Mr Jackson. But there was still more to come. I was having the time of my life!

I was surprised to see Lily start for the second half, and it was clear that as soon as the whistle blew again, she was struggling. All of her previous pace had gone, and she seemed to be disappearing from the game.

'She must still be hurt,' I said to Martha. 'Perhaps Mr Frankland didn't want to risk being a player down. After all, there's only one goal in it.'

Mr Frankland's decision appeared to be a sensible one, I wrote in my notepad, because within minutes, another Dick, Kerr player was on the ground. Poor Molly Walker had fallen heavily and from the way she was holding her leg, it looked like she had twisted her right knee.

'That's not good,' I said, flinching. My own leg throbbed in sympathy. 'Molly will have to come off.'

'This isn't fair!' Martha wailed. 'We're losing all our players!'

Molly had to be helped off the pitch. I took a photograph, marking the moment when she lifted herself from the ground, her head bent, her face pale with pain. I could feel her frustration echoing in my own belly. I could appreciate how she might feel – having to leave the game behind before it was finished, having to leave her team to continue without her.

First Lily, and now Molly.

The team were weaker. They were compromised and exposed.

I closed my eyes briefly and there I was – back there again. Swirling mists, roaring gunfire, and the echoing cries of men falling around me. Johnnie, Micky . . .

I left them exposed . . .

A rush of anger coursed through my body; it felt like a red-hot flush, beginning first in my stomach and then rushing up through my chest and into my head. It made me feel rather dizzy and sick. I put my camera down and realised that my hands were shaking.

'Are you all right, Fred?' Martha asked, her face frowning.

I stared back at her. How many times would people ask me that question? And how many times would I reply, 'I'm fine, I'm quite fine'? How long could I keep pretending like this?

I felt like I was crumbling.

I gripped the pen in my hand and took a shaky breath. I had to hold it together. This was stupid. I had a job to do. I couldn't lose it now.

'I just felt a little giddy,' I said to Martha. 'I'm probably hungry.'

'Do you want me to fetch you anything?'

Her lovely, kind face shone up at me.

'No, Martha. I'll be fine. Honestly. Just enjoy the game. Don't worry about me.'

I turned back to the pitch, my eyes still blurry, but I was determined to refocus. The action was still thrilling and luckily I found I could lose myself once again in the beautiful football being played. The Dick, Kerr Girls, although reduced to ten players, were still strong and relentless and kept up the attack. It wasn't long before they scored their second goal, and it was richly deserved. Flo set up Jennie Harris perfectly on the edge of the area and Jennie, who really was having the most spectacular game, calmly drove the ball into the top right-hand corner. The crowd roared once again in a wave of celebration.

2–0.

The Dick, Kerr Girls were clearly winning now and they kept up their attack throughout the rest of the half, only to be held back by the strong and steady central defenders on the French side. If it hadn't been for them, the score would've been far greater.

As the final whistle blew, the crowd exploded with joy and fans began to spill on to the pitch.

'Come on, Freddie,' said Martha, pulling me out of my seat. 'I want to congratulate the girls too.'

We charged forward, caught up in the surge of cheering fans who were running to each player and clapping them firmly on the back. Then a group of men picked Jennie up and carried her shoulder-high across the pitch, as if she were some kind of queen.

'Look at her!' Martha said. 'Doesn't she look grand.'

'She certainly does,' I replied, unsurprised that Jennie was getting most of the attention – after all, she had set up one goal and scored the other. There was no denying that she'd had a wonderful game.

My gaze fell on the other women – to Alice Kell, Flo, Alice Wood, and of course, Jessie. They had all been quite wonderful too. More importantly, they had all worked together as a team.

That's it, isn't it? I froze as the thought drifted past me – that was what was so special about the Dick, Kerr Girls.

They worked together. They supported one another.

They came together as one.

13

I couldn't sleep at all. My mind was a muddled fog of thoughts. The bedroom felt too small and crowded. The snores and movements from my sisters' bed only frustrated me further. I had to get away.

I slipped out of my own bed quietly, wrapped my old and frayed dressing gown around my body and padded out of the room, trying desperately to avoid the squeaky floorboard.

I couldn't go into the front room because that's where Mam and Dad were sleeping so instead I slipped into the kitchen, intending to pour myself a water to quench my dry throat.

I almost fell over Dad as I stepped into the room. It was all I could do not to shout out, I was so surprised to find him there, sat in the shadows like a ghost, hiding away from the rest of us.

'Oh!' I gripped the table and tried to ignore my pounding heart. 'I wasn't expecting to find you here.'

Dad was fully dressed and smoking a cigarette, which

was a surprise as Mam would certainly tan his hide if she caught him doing that in the house. From the weak light through the window, I could make out Dad's features – his sunken eyes, his downturned mouth; he looked like he hadn't slept for weeks.

As if reading my mind, Dad said, 'I often sit here at night, as it happens. I have trouble sleeping these days.'

His back – of course. I had guessed it still troubled him and I suspected the battered old mattress that he and Mam slept on wouldn't be helping matters.

I drew out a chair and sat opposite him. I felt weary, but still not tired. It was as if my body was exhausted, but my mind wasn't. If only I could learn to turn my mind off – that would be most of my troubles gone.

'You can't sleep either?' Dad asked, a frown etched on his face.

I hesitated. I wondered if this was the time to tell him. To admit to the ghastly nightmares that clawed into my night. Could I tell him that it was preferable to stay awake and be tormented by my troubled thoughts, then let my brain completely give into sleep and be haunted by my past? Would Dad understand? Was I even ready to talk about it all now?

I slumped back in my seat. 'I suppose I'm just getting

used to being home,' I said finally.

He studied me for a moment. It was as if his large, sad eyes could see right into me. I flinched as his gaze passed across my face.

'Freddie . . .'

'I'm fine, Dad. Don't worry.' I forced a smile, my face feeling stiff. 'I'm just tired. That's all.'

'If you're sure?'

'I'm sure.'

He nodded slowly, his sad gaze still fixed on mine for a moment or two. Then he stubbed his cigarette out in the ashtray and he reached over, his body stiff with pain. He laid a large meaty hand on my shoulder.

'I get it, lad,' he said. 'I do. Some things are difficult to say.'

As he walked out of the room, I wanted to scream for him to stay. I wanted to pull him back.

I want to tell you, Dad. I want to tell you everything.

I want you to fix me.

But, as usual, my words stayed planted inside of me, taking root.

I sat alongside Hettie on the way to the next game against the French Ladies. This was to be held at

Stockport. The girls were in fine spirits, singing songs and calling out to one another, obviously very keen to start.

'I reckon we can win this one, too,' Alice Kell declared confidently. 'We are in such good form.'

'I'd certainly like to have a run at the French defence again,' Jennie chipped in. 'They're pretty good, but I think I could get a few more past them.'

'I want at least two goals this time,' Flo declared. 'I can feel it in my waters – I'm going to score more than one.'

'I just hope I'm not injured again,' Lily Lee added from the back. 'I want a better game this time around.'

Hettie turned to me, grinning. 'It's so lovely seeing the girls this excited, isn't it? They are so thrilled about the games ahead and all the plans Mr Frankland has in mind. And to top it all, we have the return trip to France to look forward to.'

I grinned back at her. 'There certainly is a lot happening.'

'You will be able to come, won't you? On the return trip, I mean. After all, this is the first time a women's football team will be playing abroad. We are making history here. The local newspaper should want to cover it . . .'

I hesitated. 'Well – I've not run it past the editor yet.'

'But he likes the pieces you've written already?'

I nodded. 'He's really pleased. He said they were better than he expected.'

Hettie beamed. 'There you go, then. You should cover the return trip.'

'Maybe . . .' I whispered hopefully.

Hettie patted my arm. 'Well, us girls want you there. You're part of the team.'

'It's nice to know I'm appreciated.' I smiled.

Hettie looked at me over the breakfast table, her expression serious.

'I heard you shout again last night,' she whispered. 'You crept downstairs after, didn't you? Did you get any sleep after that?'

'Not really.'

'I really think you ought to see Micky,' she said softly. 'Talk to someone who understands. He should be a bit better now, able to talk?'

'I don't think it would help,' I muttered.

'But it might. How do you know, unless you try?'

'I don't know, Hettie . . .'

I was stirring the thick porridge that Mam had given us. As usual, my stomach felt like a tight little ball. I knew I had to eat – as Mam kept telling me, it was the only way I was going to get my strength back – but the thought of even taking one mouthful was a struggle. At least Mam was outside hanging washing in the yard, she wasn't there to see me fiddling with my food again.

'I didn't hear a thing,' Martha declared. 'I was having dreams too. I dreamt I was playing as a forward for the Dick, Kerr Girls. I scored the winning goal against the French team and I was lifted up high and paraded around the pitch like a lucky mascot.'

Hettie ruffled her hair. 'That could very well come true, lass. Like I told you, once the French tour is over, Mr Frankland is happy for you to start training with the girls.'

Martha's face lit up. 'I'm going to keep practising until then,' she said, pushing back her chair and running towards the door. 'In fact, I'm going to have a kick around outside now, before school.'

'You should,' Hettie said. 'Keep practising. You'll only get better and better.'

Martha rushed out of the door, a bundle of energy and excitement. We both chuckled.

Mam came back into the house looking a little stunned. 'What's that girl up to now with that blessed ball? She nearly knocked me flying,' she muttered. 'Honestly, this house and football. I feel like the game is taking over each one of you.' She looked sharply at my bowl. 'Are you not eating that, lad? We can't afford to waste food.'

I sighed and tried to shove some more porridge into my mouth. It was difficult to swallow with Mam's steely gaze fixed on me.

'You're not eating poison, Freddie. Get it down you. I swear, you're wasting away.'

Hettie, sensing the mood, turned to Mam.

'Yesterday was great fun, Mam. I wanted to tell you about it.'

Mam lowered herself into the chair carefully. She looked very tired and I noticed that she had no breakfast of her own. Mam's habits were hard to break. Even though we had money coming into the house now, I guessed she still didn't like to depend on it.

'Weren't you with Mr Frankland all day?' Mam said. 'Freddie told us you were taking the French team for a day out.'

'Yes, Mam. He wanted the French girls to see the best of Lancashire and it was grand. It was so nice to have a day away from the factory; all the girls were so excited. We all went to his house to start with. Mrs Frankland really is a dear. She made sandwiches and cakes for everyone. The French girls kept laughing, they said that us English drink too much tea.' Hettie's face lit up as she spoke.

'Well, there's nowt wrong with tea,' Mam said stoutly.

'No, of course there isn't. Anyway, then we went up to Blackpool and oh, how I loved it there. Have you ever been?'

'Aye, once, as a lass.' Mam looked wistful. 'It certainly is a lively place.'

'We all had such fun. We went along the beach and dipped our toes in the sea, even though it was very cold.' Hettie's eyes sparkled. 'Freddie, I wish you could've been there. One of the French girls lost her hat in the wind. It was blown clear off into the waves. She didn't mind, though, she just laughed and laughed. We all did.'

'It does sound fun,' I replied.

'It sounds a bit fancy, if you ask me,' Mam said. 'All this fuss for a football team. Shouldn't you be training instead?'

'This is important too, Mam. It helped us relax and have some fun. I think it helped us to form closer bonds. Do you see?'

'I do,' I said. 'I think it's a great idea.'

I thought of the quiet times in the war. The times when we tried to sleep, pressed together in our packs in the dark. Or the times when we were waiting for instruction, playing card games and singing songs.

Those had been the times when conversations had taken place, laughter had been shared and real connections had been made.

Hettie was right, the closest bonds were formed when you weren't really thinking about it. When you were relaxed.

That was when the best friendships were made.

When I arrived at work, Gordon was already stood at my desk with a smug expression cast upon his face.

'The boss wants to see you,' he said.

I frowned, wondering if I had done something wrong. I didn't think so. The report from the last Dick, Kerr game had been good, I was sure, and I was now preparing for the final game at Chelsea. After that, the games in France would follow. That would be a significant moment for the team and one that I knew the newspaper would want to cover. I only hoped that Mr Jackson would still consider me to be the best person for that job.

Mr Jackson called me in when I knocked. I sat on the chair opposite his desk and tried to control my nerves.

'Freddie, lad!' He greeted me warmly. 'How have you enjoyed covering the last few Dick, Kerr games?'

'An awful lot, sir,' I said, a little too quickly. 'Have you seen my copy?'

He nodded. 'I have indeed. I've read every word and I have to say, I'm quite impressed. You certainly write a lot better when you write about football than when you do the wanted ads.'

'I suppose it's much easier writing about something you care about . . .'

'It certainly reads that way. I didn't think I'd ever feel that interested in a bunch of women playing sport, but you make them sound rather exciting. This Alice Kell, Jessie Walmsley and Florrie . . .'

He paused.

'Redford?' I offered.

'Yes, Redford, that's it. They sound like remarkable players. I'm almost tempted to come and watch them for myself.'

'You should. You'll be even more impressed by them in real life. Honestly, I keep saying it, but they are just as good – if not better – than any men's team I've seen. And there's so much more to come.'

'Indeed?' Mr Jackson rubbed his chin. 'How so?'

'Well, Mr Frankland is looking to bring in a proper coach to help the girls in the future and, even better, in the next few weeks, Lily Parr will be joining the team – right in time for the games in France.'

'Lily Parr? Haven't I heard that name before somewhere?'

'I mentioned her to you once, sir. She's meant to be quite a prodigy. She's only fourteen and playing for St Helens. Mr Frankland said she would be the "icing on our very fancy cake".'

Mr Jackson grinned. 'Good players mean great matches, and great matches mean more interest . . . and more newspapers sold. Especially with your photographs.'

'So, everything's good then,' I said, my confidence growing. 'I can cover the Chelsea match for you and then I'll make the arrangements with Mr Frankland to travel with the girls to France. You'll have an exclusive man pitch-side, to write up the games as they happen. I can take lots of photographs, too. Good ones.'

'Oh, we'll have a man pitch-side for sure,' Mr Jackson agreed. 'But I'm afraid, Freddie lad, it won't be you.'

For a moment or two I was struck dumb. I stared back at him, my mouth slightly open, my mind racing with confused thoughts.

'Mr Jackson, sir, I don't understand – I thought I'd done a good job for you. I thought . . .'

Mr Jackson held up his hand. 'Oh, don't get into a fluster, lad. You *have* done a good job for me, a very good job. But you're a junior reporter. I took you on to learn the trade. To work your way up. I had no idea how popular the Dick, Kerr Girls would become, but now it's all I hear people talk about. It's important we get this right.'

'But I can get this right! You've seen that already . . .'

Mr Jackson smiled weakly. 'Now I understand how popular the team is, it makes sense that I ask my senior reporter to take over. He is far more experienced and much better placed to cover the games, especially those taking place abroad – that's a much bigger responsibility.'

'Gordon,' I said flatly.

'Yes, Gordon. And not to mention, it wouldn't be right to send a battle-scarred boy back to France. I don't feel comfortable with that.'

'I'm fine,' I muttered. 'My injuries aren't a burden to me and anyway, I fought in Belgium.'

France, Belgium . . . In truth, the geography didn't matter. Of course I was scared. The thought of crossing that sea again made my heart flutter. But I didn't want Mr Jackson to use that as a reason not to send me. The Dick, Kerr Girls were the one thing that had made me feel happy and useful again. I couldn't let this be taken from me.

'Please, sir,' I said, hating to hear myself beg. 'I will continue to do a good job for you. I won't let you down.'

'Freddie, I don't know . . .'

'I could still take the photographs!' I said quickly, hope growing again. 'You said mine are good. I could go with Gordon and . . .'

I could see Mr Jackson's expression hadn't changed; if anything he just looked more sorrowful.

'I've thought long and hard about this, lad. It's not been an easy decision, but the newspaper can't afford to send two men. And as Gordon quite rightly said, you are still very young. Still inexperienced . . .'

'Gordon said that?' I said coolly.

'Well, yes. We obviously discussed the issue, and Gordon and I both thought he would be in a better position to take over. Gordon has years of experience and—'

'He asked you to do this, didn't he? This was all his idea.'

'Well, that's rather by the by . . .'

I stood up. I couldn't help it. The frustration and rage was building inside of me like a volcano now. My words flew from my mouth like hot bullets.

'Gordon! The man who said that the Dick, Kerr Girls shouldn't even be playing. The man who thinks women's football is a fad and will hopefully die out soon!' I said. My voice was really rising now, but I couldn't help it. Tears were burning my eyes. 'How is he more qualified than someone who truly cares about them and actually wants them to succeed?'

'Freddie, I . . .' Mr Jackson stammered, his face now bright red.

'No sir, it's all right,' I said. 'I think I've heard enough already.'

I left the office, slamming the door behind me, leaving my dreams in tatters.

Gordon was there, of course, lingering beside my desk like a bad smell. He had a sheepish expression on his face, but there was something in his eyes that I didn't like. A glint of pleasure.

I picked up my hat and began to pull my coat on.

'Are you off already?' he asked, a smile curling on his portly red face.

'There's somewhere I need to be,' I replied coldly.

'I see. And has that been approved?'

I stared back at him. He knew that it hadn't, that

I was walking out of this office in anger and frustration. Who knew if I'd have a job when I came back? Right now, I wasn't sure I even cared.

'No,' I snapped. 'No, it hasn't.'

Gordon backed away a little.

'I know you had a talk with Mr Jackson,' he said. 'I'm guessing you're not very happy with what was said.'

'No. I'm not.'

His eyes widened. 'Well, I am sorry, lad, but that's how it works on newspapers, you know. The best reporter gets the scoops. You can't expect to waltz in here and take over the best stories.'

'I did no such thing,' I replied, buttoning up my coat. My fingers felt like fat little sausages. 'I came here to learn and to do well. I had the chance to prove myself with the Dick, Kerr Girls and I did, I proved myself. You had no interest in them. You said they were no good.'

'And I stand by that,' Gordon said, a lazy grin spreading across his face. 'I don't have to like something to report on it. I've been covering cricket matches all summer and I can't stand the game. My job as a reporter is simply to ensure that our readers get the information they want, and our readers seem to want more about the Dick, Kerr Girls.'

'You said girls shouldn't be playing football.'

'And they shouldn't. It's not fitting for a woman to be doing such things. This little fad will pass. I've heard talk. There are many that feel the same as me. This women's game can't be allowed to tarnish the men's.' He paused, tipped his head slightly to one side. 'We'll let these silly girls have their time and I will report on it and say how fun it was. And then it will end' – he clicked his fingers – 'just like that, and we can forget this nonsense ever happened.'

'I still don't understand why you want to take over, if that's the way you feel.'

'Well,' he replied smoothly, 'I've always quite fancied a trip to France.'

It was all I could do not to knock that smug smile off of his face, but instead I picked up my hat and left.

Gordon really did know nothing at all.

I found myself on the bus before I could think too much about it. The rage inside had simmered down a little. Instead, I now felt like my stomach was full of a thousand bees, squirming around. The need to get away – from the office, from anywhere that reminded of me of work – was too strong, so I leapt on the first bus I saw, paid my fare and sat myself at the back, my hat lowered so no one would recognise me.

Luckily, the bus itself was pretty empty. Two elderly women were in the seats to the right of me, gossiping loudly about their neighbour who was, apparently, 'always out at work, like no lady should be', and which was a 'disgrace in this day and age'.

I wondered idly what they would think of the Dick, Kerr Girls. There were still so many who refused to accept the world was moving on and that women's place in it might need to change too.

Wasn't it better to move on than to be left behind?

I glanced down at my fists, which were clenched upon my thighs. I knew my anger was swelling again. It was all the injustice I felt. I would have one game left with the girls. And then nasty, pig-headed Gordon would take over.

Life simply wasn't fair.

I pressed my face up against the window, watching as the images of Preston passed by. I could feel my body shaking, but I tried to ignore it. My mind was racing with thoughts. I wasn't sure what I would do next. Would I even be able to step into the office again? My outburst was surely bound to land me in hot water. Did I even want to return, knowing that my hard work had been unfairly snatched from me?

My fingers clawed at the cloth of my trousers. I knew I couldn't make any decision yet. I needed some time. I needed to think. And I also needed to do something else first.

The bus drew to a stop and I slowly got out. As I passed the two old ladies, I made myself flash them my brightest smile. They both looked up at me, blinking, obviously surprised to get my attention.

'Support your women, don't condemn them,' I said. 'This change needs to happen. Even a foolish boy like me has realised that now.'

'Oh, laddie, I don't know what—'

But I had already stepped off the bus. I walked quickly, knowing the direction I was going in. My legs felt like lead, but I made them obey. I had to do this.

A shudder came over me as soon as I saw the building up ahead.

The Moor Park Hospital.

This place had been my sanctuary the previous year. The nurses had soothed me and mended me. They had kept me warm and fed me and helped me to take my first steps with my cane across the shiny floor.

They hadn't given up on me, despite my flashes of anger and frustration. They took me in as a broken, bloodied mess and tried to piece me back to the lad I once was.

I looked up at the large windows. I knew behind one of them lay Micky Adams. He had no family close by. He was far too injured to be released yet. It would be a long time before Micky would be walking through those doors.

Micky Adams. A solider in my unit that I'd barely known, and yet, he had been there on that last fateful day. He knew what had happened. Or, at least he *thought* he knew what had happened.

All those months we had laid together side by side in the hospital and I hadn't spoken to him. I couldn't bring myself to, for fear of what he might say in return. I lied to Hettie. I told her that Micky wasn't talking at all, but that wasn't true. I heard him talking with the nurses. Micky didn't know it was me in was the bed next to him, though. His head was heavily bandaged and he couldn't move – and most days he was in a heavy drug-induced sleep. By the time he had begun to recover, I had been moved to another ward.

And I was relieved. So relieved. Because it meant I no longer had to worry about facing him.

But Hettie was right. I should try and talk to him now. That's why I came. That's why I put myself on the bus.

I knew I needed to speak to him. I needed to finally explain. For Johnnie's sake.

But as I stood on that path, a wave of nausea washed over me. I gripped the fence to try and steady myself, but it was no good.

I can't do this. I can't.

I found I was walking away, each step as heavy and laborious as they were in the mud in Belgium. My breathing was ragged, my heartbeat was fast and echoing hard in my ears.

I can't do it. I can't see Micky.

I am a coward and I always will be.

15

I am slumped on the floor of the trench. I know I should be with the men. I should be helping. But I cannot move.

I think of Johnnie. I watch as he lifts his gun ready to fire. He needs help. I should be beside him.

But I can't move.

I haven't slept properly for days, and it makes me feel dizzy and sick. I keep blinking because I can see dancing lights and shadows. I reach out to them, as if I can touch them. They look like tiny orbs or fairies drifting in front of me. The thought makes me giggle out loud.

I don't even hear the shell exploding, not immediately anyway. Instead, the orbs in front of me are driven away. There is a burst of dust and rock. I blink and lift my head.

I see flames.

I see Johnnie.

I see his face, twisted with pain as he falls away from the embankment. His gun is still clutched in his hand. Then I see his eyes, startled, unsure as he tumbles towards me. We fall together and it's almost like a dance – me gripping his arm, trying to right him – but his body is already fully in motion and drives him down hard into the ground.

Johnnie cries out, and it's an awful, sickening sound. At first, I can't look, but then, slowly, I peel my bruised and dirty body away from his.

I see poor Johnnie, his hand fluttering briefly at his side. He makes one last gasp, one last breath, and then nothing.

He has fallen . . .

And as my eyes open – as I wake from my dream – all I can think, all that I know . . . is that it should've been me. I should've been standing where he was.

It was the final game against the French girls at the Chelsea ground in London. It was a bright, sunny day which had Hettie convinced that fortune should favour us. As we sat on the coach together, she spoke excitedly of the game to come.

'I really think this will be the best yet,' she said confidently. 'Especially after the Manchester game.'

The last game at Hyde Road in Manchester had been a very tight one, resulting in a one-all draw and although I'd struggled to cover the game, as it occurred just after my meeting with Mr Jackson, I had been really impressed by both teams. In that game the French girls had been much stronger in attack and had it not been for our wonderful goalkeeper, they could have easily scored at least two more goals.

'I'm still reliving the French striker's goal celebration,' I said. 'I don't think I've seen anything quite like that before.'

'I know.' Hettie giggled. 'Who would have thought it? A complete somersault and then landing on her feet! I've never seen a male footballer do that, have you? Flo was joking that she might have to do something similar if she scores today?'

'Really?'

'Oh no, not really. Mr Frankland would be furious if she were to hurt herself from a silly celebration.' Hettie smiled. 'But it would be fun to see, wouldn't it?'

'The whole tour has been fun, really,' I said, wiping my tired eyes.

'You wait until we go to France, I bet you'll get some amazing shots there too,' Hettie replied. 'And of some of the sights as well. It really will be a wonderful experience.'

I nodded, swallowing dry air. I hadn't yet told Hettie

that I wouldn't be covering the Dick, Kerr girls after this game.

Hettie turned to me. 'It means so much to me that you're involved with the team too,' she said. 'It makes this whole experience even more special, if that's even possible. Do you see?'

'Yes, I do.'

And it made me feel sick to my stomach that it was about to end.

I tried to enjoy the game as best I could. I only wished Martha could have been there, but Mam and Dad didn't like her travelling too far. London was a faraway place to my parents, full of criminals and scoundrels. If only they could see the truth. London wasn't scary at all. In fact, the vibrancy and cheer of the crowd here reminded me of Preston.

I was sat with the other reporters, my notepad pressed against my knees and my camera beside me. The lad next to me looked a little older. He had bright ginger hair and when he smiled, I spotted a chipped tooth.

'I've heard about these Dick, Kerr Girls,' he said. 'The talk around here is that they are bleedin' good.'

His Yorkshire accent immediately threw me. I had to pause for a moment, clutching my pen tightly as I tried to gather myself. He sounded so much like Johnnie! Just for a brief second or two, I could picture Johnnie sat here beside me, taking a long swig from his water bottle and then making some bright, funny comment about the game. Oh, he would have loved all this, for sure. I dare say he would have had something to say about women playing football, but I think he would've admired them, and I know he would've been cheering as loud as anyone else. After all, Johnnie just loved football and would've liked to see it played well.

'Ey up, mate? Are you all right?' the lad beside me asked. 'I'm Jack, by the way. This is the first football game I've covered. The lads at the office weren't too bothered about it. They didn't think it would be anything special.'

'You're not from round here either, are you?' I asked.

He laughed. 'No. I'm from Leeds. I moved this way a few years ago for work.'

I shook the hand that he held out to me.

'Well, Jack, these girls are worth watching, you wait and see,' I replied. 'And I'm sorry for my reaction just then. You just remind me of someone, that's all. Someone I fought alongside.'

'Really?' He seemed interested. 'You went to war? How was it? I couldn't go, you see, on account of my flat feet.'

He lifted a booted foot as if to make a point. 'Can't say I was too bothered, though. I'm not built for fighting, me.'

I smiled wanly. 'No. To be honest, I don't think I am either.' I looked towards the pitch. 'Ey up! The game is about to start!'

The French team were clearly fired up, and soon made two early attacks on goal. They were unlucky not to score.

'Eee – this is looking tough,' Jack said. 'Do you still think our girls will win?'

'I hope so . . .' I muttered.

The Dick, Kerr Girls soon made a surging attack towards the French goal. Lily Jones took the ball neatly on the left flank and curled it high into the penalty area. Jennie Harris was there, waiting to receive it, her legs already bent, ready to spring up and control the ball on her chest. I moved forward in my seat, anticipation building. Jennie was clear on goal; this could be our first opportunity. But in a blur of speed the French defender was there. I recognised her from one of the other games, Mademoiselle Brule – she was tall and strong and not scared to throw herself into a tackle. She moved in towards Jennie and the ball, looking to dispossess her, but the two girls collided in mid-air. Jennie fell awkwardly to the floor, striking her head on the ground. My breath caught in my throat. It looked like a nasty knock. Jennie wasn't moving at all.

Mademoiselle Brule waved urgently to the officials, and almost immediately the first-aiders ran on to the pitch to check on the prone player.

Jack nudged me. 'You reckon she's knocked out?'

'It doesn't look good,' I admitted.

We watched as Jennie was carried off the pitch. I could see that her eyes were closed, and her face was pale. The remaining Dick, Kerr Girls looked sick with worry. I knew that this would shake them up good and proper. They wouldn't like to see a player go down.

'Score for Jennie!' I shouted. 'Do it for her.'

Alice Kell, who was standing nearest the line, heard me and nodded firmly. She ran to her teammates and muttered a few words of encouragement.

'They're a player down now,' Jack said. 'This will be tough.'

I nodded, my frown deepening. They had no substitute to bring on, so would have ten players against the French team's very efficient eleven. There was little doubt that the French girls looked solid today and more determined.

The rest of the half was fast-moving and end-to end, with both teams determined to make an impression. When the half-time whistle finally blew, the crowd roared with frustration. They wanted to see more.

0–0.

'We can still do this,' I whispered to Jack.

'Not quite the game I was promised,' Jack said, in quite a jovial tone. 'But still good, none the less.'

'Remember that they've lost a player to injury,' I snapped back, unable to stop myself. 'It's hard to focus when you're concerned about one of your own.'

The game restarted in much the same way as it had left off, with the Dick, Kerr Girls not looking quite their usual selves but still playing hard and fast. However, despite Hettie's earlier prediction, fortune didn't seem to be on our side this time. It wasn't long before our girl Annie Crozier inadvertently drove the ball into her own net, in a misplaced clearance. Poor Annie looked horrified as the ball flew past our goalkeeper. The crowd groaned and my stomach twisted.

'Nice goal,' Jack joked. 'If it had been at the other end.'

'It can't get much worse,' I muttered.

But I was wrong again. Moments later, our usually

confident and controlled goalkeeper, Annie Hastie, allowed a simple shot to slip through her hands. She fell to the ground in frustration and the crowd groaned again.

0–2.

The crowd began to sing songs loudly to gee the girls up.

'I never thought girls could play,' I heard one spectator say behind me.

'Indeed,' said another. 'Or kick so hard.'

I smiled to myself and made a note of their comments in my pad. I could only hope that Gordon would pay attention to this kind of thing when he took over. Maybe he would finally acknowledge that girls' football was here to stay.

And then, right before the final whistle, Lily Jones drove another perfectly angled cross into the eighteen-yard box. Flo Redford was there to receive it and with little hesitation, drove the ball sweetly into the top corner.

1–2.

It was a consolation goal, but a well-deserved one at that. As the whistle blew, the crowd roared. They didn't seem to mind the end result; it had been the game itself they had enjoyed. And the Dick, Kerr Girls seemed pleased and content with the score. Mademoiselle Brule immediately ran over to Alice Kell and kissed her firmly on the cheek. The two opponents then walked off the pitch together, arms around each other's shoulders.

'That weren't 'alf bad,' Jack admitted. 'You know, I might be tempted to watch them again. Especially if they return to London.'

'You should,' I said, my eyes glistening as I watched the teams coming together in joy, linking arms and praising one another. 'Because it really is an honour to watch.'

And I was really going to miss them.

After the match, it was time to move on to a more formal celebration. The Lord Mayor of London would be honouring both teams with a civic reception at Mansion House, and Mr Frankland was keen for me to take a photograph of the girls all dressed up in their best. Luckily, he had warned me in advance about the affair and I had brought my best suit to change into.

I managed to gather the French ladies together in the foyer of Mansion House and took a photograph as a memory for them to take home.

'This is very nice,' one French girl said in clipped

English, her eyes as round as saucers. 'It is very . . . fancy.'

'More fancy than any of us,' Flo joked back. 'But I'm going to enjoy every minute of it.'

Jessie approached me, her wide smile spread across her face as usual. Beside her were Alice Woods and Jennie, who had thankfully recovered from her injury earlier, although she was grumbling a little about her sore head.

'Isn't this wonderful?' Jessie gushed, her eyes scanning the large room. 'I can't quite believe we're here. After all, what are we? Simple factory girls! And now look at us!'

'We've been welcomed by all sorts,' Alice whispered to me. 'I've already met all the top brass – famous entertainers and a really important politician. Apparently.' She screwed up her face. 'He was a bit stuffy, though.'

Jennie giggled. 'Well, we are important too, girls. We are one of the best female football teams in the country, about to go to France and conquer them there too!'

'Cheers to that,' Alice said, holding up her glass. 'I can't wait. I only wish Lily Parr could be here now to see this. She wouldn't believe it, she really wouldn't. I don't think I've ever been anywhere as posh.'

'Lily is joining in the next week, isn't she?' I asked. 'You must be excited?'

Alice nodded, her smile spreading. 'She can't wait.' She paused. 'Oh, Freddie, you'll have to write a special piece on her. She's so young, yet so talented.'

I bowed my head a little. I would be there, at Deepdale training ground, when Lily Parr arrived, because Mr Frankland wanted me to take a new team photograph with Lily included. But I wasn't ready to tell them that soon I would not be covering their adventures any more. It still felt so unfair. I only wished I had confidence in Gordon to do a good job.

Jessie laid her hand gently on my arm. 'You always look so troubled, Freddie. You should be happy. The Dick, Kerr Girls and all that ride with us are on the up.'

'Jessie, I . . .'

It wasn't the time to say it. This night wasn't about me. Instead, I managed a weak smile.

'I hope you're right, Jessie.'

'Oh, I am Freddie. I just know it.'

We have to get out.

The gunfire is exploding around us. Micky is shouting, he is telling me we have to move.

I tug myself away from Johnnie. His body rolls into the mud, his face pressing into the dirt. I move his head gently. Even though I know he's gone, I can't stand to leave him here in the muck.

We never leave our brothers . . .

'Johnnie.'

I try to pull at him, but his body is heavy. My feet slip and slide further in the mud.

Micky shouts again.

'We need to move. NOW!'

I can't leave him, I can't leave a brother. I promised.

'FREDDIE!'

'WE CAN'T LEAVE HIM!'

I try and pull him again, but he's too heavy. I'm too weak. Micky is beside me now.

'I'm sorry, lad.' Micky's hand rests briefly on my back.

'He's gone. You have to let him go.'

'But—'

'Freddie. I'm sorry.'

My fingers find Johnnie's inside pocket. Before I know what I'm doing, I'm taking out the photograph. The picture of his Betsy. Just like I said I would.

'I can't tell her,' I whisper to his silent face. 'I can't tell her about this, Johnnie.'

I can't . . .

'FREDDIE! MOVE!'

Micky's cry drives me to action. I don't want to go. And yet, I find my feet moving away from the trench and away from my friend. I am crawling over the edge, my fingers digging into the rough.

I don't want to leave him. Not there. It's too ugly. Too undignified.

But as I stumble into the battlefield, I don't know what else to do.

I don't want to die here either.

I'm scared.

Micky is in front of me, just to my left. There is gas around us, in thick, choking clouds. I can't see properly. I am staggering. My gas mask is heavy on my face. I try to breathe.

Screams are everywhere, fallen men. I don't want to see

and yet my eyes make me. I see their bodies on the floor. I see death everywhere. It is so close now, I can taste it.

The next explosion of gunfire is the loudest yet. I'm sent spinning to the ground. My head snaps briefly to the side. I catch sight of Micky; I see the flames licking at his clothes. I see the thick gas swarming towards the both of us.

And then, as I hit the floor, I feel the pain flaring in my leg. The exhaustion flooding my body. I glance down at my hand and see that I'm still clutching the photograph.

Finally, I see nothing.

And I'm glad.

It was the day of Lily Parr's arrival and, as usual, I had been unable to get much sleep. I ended up lying in bed, staring at the early morning shadows on the ceiling.

After a bit, I decided that staring into space was doing me no good at all, so I went downstairs for a drink. It was cool and fresh in the kitchen. I sat at the table, sipping at my water, trying to gather together my thoughts. My dreams had been fragmented this time.

I wondered if this was how madness began. Was this just the start for me? Would I ever sleep again?

'What are you doing, sitting there?'

I looked up. Dad was standing in the doorway,

dressed ready to go to work at the docks. I had forgotten he would be leaving around this time.

'Honestly lad, it's doing you no good moping around like this,' he continued as he moved into the kitchen. 'You'll make yourself sicker.'

I lowered my head, not knowing what to say. But Dad continued anyway.

'When I hurt my back, son, don't you think I was angry with the world? Every day now, it's a struggle. At work I sometimes want to scream in pain, I long to just down tools and leave, but what good would that do me, eh?' He sat down opposite, began to ram his feet into his boots, groaning as he did so. 'It's no help sitting around thinking about what ifs or wishing things were different. We need to move forward, lad. It's the only way.'

'I'm trying,' I muttered. I rubbed at my face. 'But my sleep . . .'

'The pain is keeping you awake, is it? I suppose we could find out if there's anything stronger you can take—'

'No,' I interrupted. 'It's not the pain, Dad. Sometimes that's bad, but it's not what's keeping me awake. It's the dreams. It's the memories of what I saw out there. It won't leave me.'

Dad's eyes found mine. There was a softening, and for a brief moment I felt an understanding sweep between us. He sighed gently, his shoulders slumping forward.

'Aye, son. It must've have been bad.' He chewed on his lip, considering me for a moment or two. 'I don't like to think of the things you saw. You're still so young, too young . . . You know my thoughts on war – I don't approve of it. Not at all. And, if I'm honest, I'm not sure I'll ever properly understand what you went through.'

'I don't think I understand either.'

'Maybe you're not meant to,' he said softly. 'Sometimes things don't make sense.' His eyes lowered. 'I dunno, son. I like to think hurt can make us stronger. It helps us to be better people in the end.'

'You think so?'

'Aye, I do.' His gaze found mine again. It was warm and familiar. 'And I'm proud of you, son. I'm proud of you for always doing what you think is best.'

'It's means a lot, Dad – you saying this,' I whispered.

'Perhaps you should have a drink before bed.' He chuckled softly. 'A shot of whisky always works for me.'

'Thanks. I'm not sure it would for me, though.'

'Aye.' He got up slowly from his chair, his gaze still fixed on mine. 'I just want you to find something that works, lad. I want you better. Or, at least, as better as you can be. I just want my boy back.'

And then, slowly, as if he had the weight of the world on his shoulders, he left the room.

I was still very tired as I walked with Hettie and Martha to the training ground, but at least the arrival of Lily had put in me in good spirits. It was also helping me to forget my talk with Dad that morning.

Martha had insisted on coming. This was her chance to meet a new star player. She wasn't going to be left behind!

'Do you think Lily's friendly?' Martha asked, as we approached the gates.

'Oh, I'm sure she is,' Hettie replied confidently. 'I've heard nothing but good things.'

Lily had already started working with most of the girls on the factory floor, but Hettie had been too busy in Mr Frankland's office to go down and formally meet her. This was the first time Lily was training with the girls, so it would be an opportunity for Hettie, and the rest of the team, to finally see what this young player was all about.

As we approached, I picked out Lily straight away.

She was fairly tall and stocky with short, neatly combed dark hair and a serious expression on her face.

'Hello!' Hettie said brightly, as we walked over. 'I'm Hettie. I help Mr Frankland with the running of the club and do all the boring bits that he doesn't like.' She laughed nervously, then indicated towards me. 'This is my brother, Freddie. He's a reporter for the local paper; he's been following the girls' games. He's also a photographer.'

I tipped my hat politely at Lily. 'I'll be taking some photographs today, if that's all right, and perhaps later, we could have a quick conversation?'

Lily nodded. I noticed that her eyes were darting between me and Hettie. She did look rather nervous and I wondered how overwhelming this must be for her. She was only fourteen, after all.

'And I'm Martha!' my little sister interrupted suddenly, and proceeded to curtesy to Lily like she was the Queen of England or something. The girls all burst into laughter.

'Oh, look at that, Lil,' Alice said. 'You've already got your own personal fan.'

'I didn't realise we were amongst royalty,' Flo said, fanning her face dramatically.

'We shall have to mind our P's and Q's!' Jennie declared.

Martha had turned a bright shade of red. She righted herself and looked quite put out. I was about to say something kindly to her, that the girls were only being silly, when Lily stepped forward and placed her hand gently on Martha's shoulder.

'Never mind them,' she said, smiling. 'It's great to meet you, too, Martha. Do you like football, then?'

'I do. I do!' Martha said. 'I play all the time. Hettie says I will be able to train with the Dick, Kerr Girls after your tour.'

Lily's smile spread. She clearly wasn't troubled by her teammates' teasing. 'That's great news. And if you're a football fan, I already know I like you.'

It was pretty clear that Lily Parr was going to fit in just fine.

I took a few photographs that morning. The first was the updated team shot, where the Dick, Kerr Girls looked even more complete with Lily Parr standing among them. It was like she was the final piece of the jigsaw, waiting to be slotted in.

As the girls stood facing me in their matching striped

kits, their arms folded and their bright faces smiling towards the camera, I felt a surge of happiness. Mr Frankland had been right all those months ago. This team was growing into something huge, and it was so wonderful to see it taking shape right in front of me.

A little later, I took Lily to one side to take an individual photograph of her. She seemed a little unsure.

'Why me?' she asked, a little self-consciously.

'Well – you're the new player,' I began, then lowered my voice a bit. 'And anyway, it helps me. I'm still learning how to take these shots well. Mr Frankland wants me to become an expert. So, really – you are doing me a favour.'

She nodded, her expression serious. I took the shot quickly, not wanting to make her feel uncomfortable for too long.

'I'm sorry,' she said. 'I'm just not used to being made a fuss of like this. Photographs and everything . . .'

'You don't like the attention on you?' I asked carefully.

'Oh, it's not that,' she said. 'I just like to get things done. I want to be on the pitch with the football, not standing around smiling for a camera. No offence.'

'None taken,' I said with a smile.

'Ey up, Lil! We can see you blushing from here!'

I looked up. Alice Woods and Jessie were approaching

us. Jessie strode over to Lily and gently squeezed her arm.

'You'll have to get used to this attention, lass. You've been the talk of the town these past few weeks. Everyone's been excited about you coming.'

Lily ducked her head a little, tucking her hair behind her ears. 'Nobody should be talking about me. I'm really nowt special,' she said. 'It's the team that matters, not me.'

'And now you're part of it, Lil,' Alice said. 'And we couldn't be more excited.'

Jessie turned to me. 'Freddie, you must be excited too? The French tour is nearly here.'

Alice's face brightened. 'Oh, can you believe it? Our first international tour. It won't be long before we are touring the world!'

'I've always wanted to do that,' Lily said quietly. 'See the world.'

'And you will,' Jessie said. 'We all will. It's so exciting.' She hesitated. Her bright eyes were fixed on mine again. Her smile suddenly dropped.

'Freddie? Aren't you excited too?'

I sighed, my body feeling heavy again. I rubbed at my sore leg.

'I'm not going,' I said finally. 'I'm only here today to

take team photographs for Mr Frankland. I'm no longer covering the games for the newspaper, someone else is taking over.'

'Someone else?' Jessie repeated. 'Who?'

'Gordon,' I said flatly. 'Apparently he is more experienced. My editor has concerns that I won't cope with the travelling. He thinks I'm too young, too new, too injured.'

Too damaged.

'That's rubbish,' Lily burst in. 'Your injury should have nothing to do with it.'

'Exactly,' Jessie said, her face flushing. I could see her own scar now, standing out on her skin. She brushed it quickly with her fingertips and a soft frown settled. 'I can't believe they are doing this to you. Is that the man we met at the office? He's an ignorant pig. He doesn't even like women's football!'

Alice frowned. 'If he doesn't like our game, he shouldn't be writing about it.'

'He only wants to do it because you're becoming successful and popular,' I said. 'Besides, he gets a free trip to France.'

'Stuff that!' Ali said, looking quite put out. 'That's not right. You need to put a stop to it.'

'You really do, Freddie,' Jessie said. 'You can't let bullies like Gordon get their own way. Go back to the newspaper. Tell the daft editor that you need to carry on writing for us. Tell him that you must! Make him see that you're the best person for the job.'

'And what if he doesn't listen?'

Jessie's smile slowly returned. 'Well . . . I'm sure he wouldn't want a group of angry women turning up at his door, would he?'

'You'd do that?' I stuttered.

'Of course we would, wouldn't we girls?' She turned to Alice and Lily.

Lily nodded keenly in reply.

Alice smiled at me. 'Us girls have to fight all our lives, Freddie. We're used to it. We fight all the time.' She paused. 'But maybe you need to start fighting back, too?'

Her words stung, but she didn't mean it that way, of course.

Lily and Alice wandered off to be with the other girls and I was left standing there with Jessie, feeling quite small and beaten.

I needed to fight back. It was the right thing to do.

But I wasn't very good at fighting, was I? I was just good at running. At hiding.

Jessie moved closer to me.

'Alice was only talking about the newspaper.'

'I know.'

'She doesn't know about your experience in the war.'

'I know.'

'Freddie, you look so pale – like you're about to faint.'

'I know . . .'

She sighed. I looked up, hoping she wouldn't see the tears in my eyes.

'You need to get help, Freddie. You can't put these demons to rest on your own.'

'I'm trying. I am.'

I felt so weak. So daft, standing here, about to cry in front of a girl I barely knew. *What must she think of me?*

'Freddie . . . will you tell me what happened? In the war? What is it that upsets you so much? I might be able to help . . .'

I went to open my mouth. The words were there, they were waiting to come out.

Would I feel lighter if I spoke?

Freer?

Would I finally sleep?

'I—'

'Jessie!'

The shout came from across the park. The girls had started their training. Alice Kell was standing, hands on hips, looking over at us. They needed Jessie.

'I can tell them to wait,' she said.

'No. The girls need you. You mustn't let them down.'

She flashed me a concerned look. 'As long as you're sure?'

'I am. I am. We can talk after.'

I watched as she ran back towards the girls and then carefully, I gathered my things and turned away. The moment had passed.

Jessie was right. I needed to sort out this mess, once and for all.

I needed to face up to my mistakes.

I sat on the bus in a daze, Alice's words replaying in my head.

Maybe you need to start fighting back, too ...

I got off the bus slowly and crossed the road towards the huge, imposing building in front of me. This time I did not hesitate outside the gates. This time, I made myself walk in, urging my feet forward.

I was back outside Moor Park hospital.

As I approached the main doors, I felt a familiar

flutter of unease in my stomach. I had been very sick when they first brought me here – so unwell. This place had started the process of fixing me back together, but there were bits of me that were still broken.

I knew that now.

I pushed open the main door and walked into the foyer. I was immediately greeted by a young, friendly nurse.

'Can I help you, sir?' she asked.

'Yes. Yes, I hope so,' I replied nervously. 'I'm here to see an old comrade, Micky – Micky Adams. Can you take me to him, please?'

17

When I'd been discharged from Moor Park last year, Micky had spent his days asleep in his bed – so I was surprised when the nurse walked me through to the main rest room to see him.

'It's nice of you to come,' she said breezily. 'Micky doesn't get many visitors.'

Micky was sat by the window in a high-backed chair. I saw straight away that most of his body was still dressed in bandages. He looked up on my approach and I was relieved to see a smile light up his unblemished face. The nerves that had been coiling around my stomach like hungry snakes immediately melted away.

'Freddie lad!' he said loudly. 'You came back. I never saw you before you left this place.'

'I'm sorry. I should have said goodbye,' I replied, feeling ashamed.

'It doesn't matter, I was asleep most of the time anyway. The drugs they give you really knock you out, eh?' He gestured towards the chair opposite. 'Sit down!

It's good to see you. It really is.'

I lowered myself down awkwardly into the seat. I could feel Micky's eyes upon me. He nodded briefly.

'That leg still giving you trouble, eh?'

I rubbed at it, as if that could take the sharp pain away. 'A bit.'

'And you got a bit of a bang to your head, so I heard.' He sniffed, scratched at his heavy moustache. 'That damn war has a lot to answer for.'

'How are you?' I asked cautiously.

Micky shrugged. 'I got burnt pretty bad from that shell, as you know. Mainly on my chest and arms.' He held up his heavily bandaged hands. 'I guess you could say my piano-playing days are over. The nurses say I will be here some time longer and then I hope to go to my aunt in the country. My mam is ill, so it's really the best place for me to be.' He coughed loudly, a dry rattle that seemed to shake his entire body. 'The gas got right into my lungs. They think the country air might be better for me. Who knows . . .'

'The gas got me too,' I said softly. 'My lungs don't feel the same.'

The gas had come after the shell exploded, as me and Micky had crawled out of the trench trying to escape.

I couldn't forget the feeling of it seeping into my lungs, slowly choking me. My hand instinctively touched my throat.

'We really took a hammering, didn't we,' Micky replied. 'But we survived, lad, and plenty didn't.'

I lowered my head a little; my other hand still massaging my sore leg. Words were tumbling around inside of me and it was difficult to find the right ones to use next.

'Micky . . .' I started hesitantly. 'Micky, I'm sorry. I should have come to see you sooner. When I knew you were awake, when I knew you were talking, I should've come back.'

'So why didn't you?' His tone was kind, not cold, but I still felt a shiver curl down my spine.

'I – I was scared, Micky. What happened that day to Johnnie, it was my fault. I should have been stood next to him. Instead, I froze, I hid behind you all . . .'

'No.' His voice was firmer now. 'No. You don't need to say this.'

'But Johnnie died because of me. And maybe you wouldn't have been so badly injured if I had done what I was supposed to d—'

'No!' His voice was louder now; it cut through my

speech and made me freeze. 'No, Freddie, this is no good. You need to stop this, now.'

'But I can't.' I realised I was shaking. I gripped my leg tighter to try and regain control. 'I keep having dreams – nightmares, I suppose. I relive it all. It's like my mind is taunting me. Telling me what I did wrong.'

'I have those dreams too,' Micky said, his voice much softer now. 'Oh my god, the dreams. We all have them here, Freddie. You must remember? The cries at night. The men that refuse to sleep.'

I paused for a moment to consider this. How had I forgotten? Micky was right. I had woken many times to wounded men shouting out in the night. At the time, I had assumed it was because of the pain from their injuries, but what Micky was saying made sense. We were all suffering with what we had seen.

'You're not alone, lad. You're not the only one.' Micky flinched as he shifted in his chair. 'And do you know what? I doubt your actions would've made any difference that day. The Germans ambushed us from all sides. We would've been caught, no matter where we were stood.' He paused. 'There's no point dwelling on it. It doesn't help things.'

'But Johnnie might have lived.'

'Perhaps he would have, but perhaps he wouldn't.' Micky's voice was flat now. 'Perhaps all three of us would be in our graves and three families would be weeping as a result of it.'

'But I left him . . .' I whispered. 'I didn't take him with us.'

'Freddie.' His voice, quiet and low. 'He was dead, lad. That shell got him bad. You know that. He would've died more or less instantly, I reckon. I doubt he would've known a thing.'

My head dropped. I couldn't speak; everything felt lodged in my throat. I felt like I might choke.

'Freddie,' Micky said. 'You must put these thoughts to bed now. What's done is done. Focus on recovering – that's what I'm doing. God knows, I get angry sometimes. I get upset; I get bitter. But what good does that do me, eh?' He sighed and another angry cough ripped through his body. He swiped his hand across his lips before continuing. 'I will not let the war win. I'm still here. I'm still breathing – just. I will not let it beat me.'

I lifted my head and took in the sight of my fellow soldier. I saw the determined tilt of his jaw and the angry flare of light behind his eyes. Yes, he was injured, but he was still the brave, strong man I had fought beside.

And he didn't blame me.

'Freddie,' Micky said finally, his voice gentle now, his gaze soft. 'Promise me you will not let this beat you too. You need to keep going. You need start living. For the sake of all of us. For Johnnie and the others who didn't make it. Don't let their lives be in vain.'

'But it's hard . . .' I whispered.

'I'm not saying these feelings will go away. I don't think it will ever stop. But . . .' He paused. 'But I do think time will help. It will get easier. It will.'

There was a silence between us. I took in what he said. I sat back in the chair and realised the tightness in my stomach had reduced a little. My breathing was calmer.

'I have his photograph,' I said. 'Of his wife, Betsy. I took it that day.'

'Really?' Micky raised an eyebrow. 'What will you do with it?'

'Johnnie wanted me to contact Betsy, to find her and tell her what happened. But I can't. Not yet.' I shuddered. 'It's still in my drawer. I've not taken it out since I've been back. I can't bring myself to.'

'You'll do what's best in the end, lad. I'm sure,' Micky said quietly. 'There's no hurry.'

'I suppose.'

'You need to think like Johnnie. Think what he would want you to do. He wouldn't like you sitting here, worrying yourself into an early grave. I'm sure he'd want you to be the best version of yourself. He'd want you to live the life he would have. He would hate for you to throw it away.'

I looked at Micky and nodded softly. He was right, of course.

Johnnie would demand nothing less.

I got the bus back into the town centre, thinking about my early days on the army base when Johnnie would sit next to me and try to calm my nervous thoughts. He'd pat my leg and tell me firmly to keep my chin up and straighten my shoulders so that I looked taller. He'd tell me to stand up to any of the other lads who might be teasing me or saying mean words because I was young and shy.

The newspaper office was quiet when I entered. It was almost the end of the day. I was relieved. Although I had been building up my confidence on the way, I wasn't sure I could face lots of people. Looking around, I quickly saw that Gordon was in Mr Jackson's office. I hesitated – could I really do this? But then I saw Johnnie in my mind's eye. It was almost as if he was stood right in front of me, his arms folded and a stern expression on his face. *Stand up for yourself!*

I took a shaky breath, trying desperately not to cough, and marched into the editor's office. They both looked up, startled at first, but Gordon's shocked face was soon replaced by his familiar snide grin.

'Back so soon, lad?' he said. 'We thought we'd upset you.'

'Well, you had,' I said. I turned my attention to Mr Jackson, who was staring up at me curiously, as if he couldn't quite work me out.

'Sir,' I said, as confidently as I could. 'You've made a mistake taking me off the Dick, Kerr games.'

Gordon immediately scoffed, but Mr Jackson held up a hand to silence him.

'And why do you think that, Freddie?'

'I *know* it,' I replied. 'I'm the best man for the job and I think you know it too, really. I also know that Gordon here has tried to convince you otherwise, but no other local reporter knows the girls like I do. Gordon certainly doesn't. He simply wants a free trip to France.'

Gordon's cheeks flushed. 'That's not the case. You know I admire the girls. I know as much as anyone.'

'All right then,' I challenged him. 'What's the name of their goalkeeper?'

'I – er . . .' He coughed. 'This is daft. I can't say off the top of my head.'

'Annie Hastie,' I told him. 'Another, then? What's the name of the new coach they've just appointed to help the team?'

'I can't be expected to know that!' Gordon was flustered.

'But I do! George Birkenshaw.' I turned to my editor. 'Sir, I'm privy to all kinds of inside information due to my sister working with the team. I'm friends with Mr Frankland and most of the girls – even my littlest sister is being teed up to train with them. You won't find a reporter with better connections. They all trust me. They all like me.' I paused, took a breath. 'And what's more, I'm a good photographer. You've said so yourself. You get two for one with me.'

'Hmmm.' He seemed to be considering my words. 'But I still worry about you going back to the place where you fought. It might upset you.'

'What about it? I'll be perfectly fine. My sister will be with me. There is nothing about my health that would prevent me going. And anyway, as I told you before,

I fought in Belgium, not France – like your son.' I let those words hang between us for a moment. 'Sir, I can assure you, I will be fine.'

'Mr Jackson, this is madness. You can't send a junior to such an important tour,' Gordon shouted.

'Maybe not.' Mr Jackson eyed me, and then a small smile crept on to his face. 'But there is a first time for everything, eh Freddie?'

It was almost as if I could feel Johnnie's hand clapping me hard on the back.

Go on, Freddie!

'Thank you, sir.' I caught Gordon's glare as I turned to leave the room. 'You won't regret this.'

Later that evening I stood beside Hettie and watched the girls train. I felt lighter somehow, as if a huge weight had been removed from inside of me.

The girls also seemed to have extra energy. It was only a few weeks until their French tour. They had a few domestic games to play and then the real challenge would begin. Their new coach, George Birkenshaw, was there, keen to put the girls through their paces. He was young and driven, with a booming voice that echoed across the field.

'There's going to be lots of training to help the girls prepare for France,' Hettie told me. 'Mr Frankland has asked for the help of some ex-footballers to share their skills and experience. I think Bob Holmes is coming to the next session and then Johnnie Morley and Billy Grier.'

My ears pricked up. These were impressive names! Bob Holmes was one of the original Preston North End players, nicknamed the 'Invincible' because he was so good.

'It just shows the reputation the girls now have, that they can attract professional coaching,' I said.

Hettie grinned. 'It's almost as if we are being taken seriously . . .'

'Oh, I think people are definitely taking you seriously now.'

Hettie's entire face was lit up like a beacon. I realised, in that moment, how completely happy this team had made her. 'This really is something special,' she said finally. 'That's the one thing I've come to realise. There really is nothing as special as the Dick, Kerr Girls.'

The weeks passed in a most excitable flurry and, before we knew it, the French tour was upon us. I had been kept busy at work and managed in the most part to avoid more evil glares from Gordon, who seemed to have accepted that I had won this most recent battle. I was also feeling a little brighter. The dreams still haunted me, and I still had moments of waking in sheer terror, but I think I was becoming more used to both now. Micky's words kept replaying inside of me, giving me a new kind of determination.

'I wish I could go to France too,' Martha complained.

'Maybe next time, Marth,' Hettie said gently. 'But when we come home, we will tell you everything. There will be so many stories!'

'You promise? You promise to tell me *everything*?'

'Of course we will. And hopefully, in a few years, you'll be one of the girls playing in an international tour. Wouldn't that be wonderful?'

Martha clapped her hands against her chest. 'Yes. It really would be.'

Dad was in his armchair, listening to us. 'So,' he said. 'The reporter job of yours is giving you the opportunity to travel . . . That's what you always wanted to do, son,' he said, smiling.

His beady eyes seemed to be watering a little; he blinked slowly. 'You'll look after our Hettie out there, won't you? In France? I worry – you know that, don't you? I just worry.'

'I know,' I replied carefully. 'And I will look after her, Dad. There really is nothing to fret about.'

He sat back in his chair. 'And now young Martha tells me she will soon be flaunting her ambitions and fancies too?'

'She's a good footballer, Dad.'

'I don't doubt she is,' he said. 'And I don't doubt that training with the team will make her even better. It's just . . .' His voice drifted for a moment. I waited patiently. I knew the words would find their way to him. They always did, eventually. 'It's just, change is hard for an old goat like me, but I'm trying, Freddie. I'm trying to be a better person.'

I stared back at him. I felt like my insides were swelling up; my throat felt dry and tight and I had to fight back a cough.

'So am I, Dad. So am I.'

**

On Thursday the 28th of October, 1920, the big day arrived. As the morning dawned and I woke, the realisation immediately hit me – history was about to be made, and Hettie and I were about to be part of it.

We were in a rush to get to the factory, where we would be picked up and driven to the station. Hettie was in a mild panic, convinced that she had forgotten to pack something vital and Mam was fussing at us, as the sudden reality that we were both going away hit her.

'I don't like to think of it,' she admitted. 'You're so far away if there's any bother. And both so young.' Her gaze drifted up and down my body, as if she were assessing me. 'Do you really think you're strong enough for this, Freddie? It's a long journey and you already look done in.'

I tried to ignore the usual thump of a headache behind my eyes and the fuzzy feeling that lack of sleep left me with. I was also sick with nerves. This tour wasn't just important for the girls. It was important for me, too. I had a lot to prove. I didn't want Mr Jackson to regret his decision, and I knew Gordon would laugh in my face if I was to mess this up.

'I'll be fine, Mam. I promise.' I kissed her powdered cheek, remembering that she had worn this same worried expression on the day I had left for war. 'Give Dad a hug from us too.'

Dad had already left for work and I was actually sad not to see him to say goodbye.

'I will, lad,' Mam said. 'I know he will miss you both terribly.'

Martha ran to us, wrapping her arms tightly around my waist. 'Remember, I want to hear every detail,' she said.

'I will write it all down, so I don't forget,' I replied, smiling. 'After all, that's what I'm there for.'

'Tell Jennie I want her to score lots of goals; she's still my favourite.' She untangled her arms from my body and stepped back. 'And Lily Parr – I like her too. I can't believe she's only a little bit older than me.'

'It just shows you what you can achieve when you put your mind to it,' Hettie said, bending to kiss Martha on the cheek. 'Make sure you keep practising while we are gone. The training will be tough when the girls get back and if you want to take part, you need to be tough too.'

'I will be,' Martha said. 'I can still run rings around the boys on the street.'

Hettie turned to me and grinned. 'It won't be long until you're writing about your own little sister.'

I glanced down at Martha, thinking about how small she had been when I had left to fight. So much had changed in that time. We had all changed. We had all grown in different ways.

'Nothing would make me prouder,' I said.

We left the factory in a motor charabanc, decorated with Union Jacks and French flags. The sixteen players sat on either side of the large vehicle, with some of the support staff, including Hettie, Mr Frankland and George Birkenshaw standing at the back. I offered to stand, as any gentleman would have, but Hettie ordered me to sit on account of my leg.

'You need to rest it as much as you can,' she said. 'Remember, I promised Mam we'd look after each other.'

I found myself pressed up quite tightly between Jessie and Jennie, which was a little uncomfortable. I wasn't used to sitting so close to girls that weren't my sisters. But Jessie and Jennie didn't seem to care – like the rest of the team, they were too busy leaning over the side of the charabanc and waving.

We were to travel up to London first by train, and then stay overnight at the Bonnington Hotel, which sounded very fancy. After our overnight stay, we were to get another train down to Dover, where we would board a ferry to take us across to Calais in France. From there, we would pick up a final train to Paris. In all, we were facing quite a journey.

'We must go out in London tonight,' Jennie said, leaning back inside. 'Most of the girls want to see the London Palladium. You'll come with us, won't you, Freddie?'

'You try and stop me.' I smiled.

Jessie nudged me, her eyes busy scanning the streets in disbelief. 'Look at all the people out there. I can't believe they are all here for us!'

It really was impressive to see the crowds line the streets in this way. Preston was coming together as a city to support their girls.

'It's amazing, isn't it,' Hettie said behind me. 'To think, just a few years ago people around here were against the team. Looking at the numbers out today, I would think most have changed their minds.'

'It really seems that way,' I agreed.

We arrived at the train station in good spirits. Most of the girls were laughing and joking amongst themselves. I glanced over at Lily Parr. If there were any nerves inside this girl, she wasn't showing it. She was busy swapping hats with Alice Woods and laughing brightly as her hair got messed up.

I gathered the team together. I wanted a photograph to mark this quite wonderful day and it seemed apt to take it outside of the station. One of the girls plucked a small boy holding a French flag from the crowd and everyone smiled at the camera, their eyes shining with excitement. Mr Frankland would not be pleased if we missed the train, so I took the picture quickly. I knew immediately it would be a poignant one – this was a group of women about to make history.

Once the flashbulb exploded, Alice Kell pumped her fist into the air. 'This is it, girls! Here we go!'

The others burst into a cheer of agreement. This was really it. The next part of the Dick, Kerr journey was beginning.

19

It was a bright, beautiful Saturday morning in France. I met Hettie early in the hotel reception, ready for our day ahead.

'Are you all right, Freddie?' she queried. 'You were awfully quiet on the train journey last night.'

'I'm fine.' I smiled. 'I was just enjoying the view.'

I had been busy staring out at the passing French countryside, but I hadn't really been enjoying it at all. A twitchy, uneasy feeling remained within me. Would I see more damage as we ventured deeper into France? Would it bring back memories that I was trying to supress? Luckily, these parts of the countryside weren't too badly damaged, and for the most part we flew by open fields and vales. It was quite breathtaking at times and I tried to relax a little and enjoy the views. This was, after all, meant to be an adventure!

At one point we had passed a cemetery and Mr Frankland had grimly remarked that it was a military graveyard. My skin had turned ice cold as the train drew past the rows and rows of graves, with beautiful floral arrangements marking each one out. I knew many British soldiers would be lying there, soldiers far unluckier than I. It made me feel a mixture of gratitude and guilt, which was a heady, sickly mix. Hettie had started talking about something else then, something to do with the plans for when we were in Paris – but I felt unable to join in and instead had pressed my face up against the window and allowed my thoughts to drift.

Why on earth had I come back?

Maybe Mr Jackson was right. I was too weak, too battle-scarred to do this job.

Was I going to mess it all up and prove Gordon right?

Would this horrible feeling ever go away?

It was all I could do not to cry out aloud. To pull on Hettie's arm and beg for her to take me back home again. To the safety of Mam, Dad and Martha.

No, I hadn't been fine at all.

'Did you sleep better?' Hettie asked now, taking my arm as we walked out of the hotel towards the rest of the team, who were waiting outside.

'I did, actually,' I lied. 'I think the journey wore me out.'

'Me too!'

'I'm glad we have a day off today,' I said. 'It might take my mind off Mr Jackson for a moment or two.'

Hettie squeezed my arm. 'Are you still worried about that? You know that you can write a good report on us.'

I half-smiled. 'I suppose it's more Gordon I'm worried about. You know, he's just waiting for me to make a mistake.'

'Well, it's good that you won't, then!'

The girls looked up as we approached them. They all looked energised and excited after a good night's sleep.

'Ey up!' Alice called out. 'We were beginning to give up on you two.'

'Freddie was late down.' Hettie smiled at me. 'The poor lamb likes his beauty sleep.'

If only.

'I was sorting my camera out!'

Jessie laughed. 'That's what you're telling us! I bet you just rolled out of bed.'

Lily yawned loudly at this. 'Well, I know I did.'

We started to walk down the main street, the girls still laughing and giggling. Not that I minded. It was nice to be in light-hearted company.

'Did you hear Lily complaining about the food last night?' Hettie whispered to me as we walked to our first tourist stop, the Chamber of Deputies. 'I don't think she's a fan of French cuisine.'

I stifled a laugh, as Lily wasn't too far ahead and I didn't want her to think we were being unkind. It was already clear that she spoke her mind plainly, despite her young age.

'What was it she said again?' I whispered. '"I don't know what the bloody hell this is, but I'm starving. I could eat a scabby old donkey."'

'She's so funny,' Hettie said warmly. 'I'm really glad she's joined the team. She makes it even better.'

The tour of Paris was very busy. I managed to use my camera a great deal, taking pictures of the Champs Élysées and even managing to get a shot of the Arc de Triomphe after a mammoth climb up the two hundred and eighty steps. It took an age because of my gammy leg and it didn't half throb after, but I was determined to make it to the top.

'This will get us fit for the match,' Jessie said, puffing her cheeks out.

'It'll get us fit, or put our backs out,' Lily shot back, grinning. 'Either way, it's worth it for the view. Just take a look. We are on top of the world!'

We stopped for a moment then, just to look around and take in the view.

'You're right, Lily.' Jessie said, breathing out hard. 'We really are on top of the world.'

We stayed awhile at Notre Dame – a few of the girls were fascinated by the spot where Napoleon married Josephine. The cathedral itself was unsettling. All of the stained glass in the windows had been removed during the war to protect it from the bombing raids. It felt quite eerie and bleak now, like standing in a building that was really only half there.

'It's good they took measures to protect the building,' Hettie said, squeezing my hand.

'It's just sad that they ever had to,' I said, my eyes still fixed on the empty space where the glass should've been. 'This poor building was at risk, and for what? I still don't really understand what it was all about.'

Hettie gently guided me away. The others were already streaming outside, ready to move on.

'We just have to deal with the here and now.' Her voice was soft and comforting. 'The sun is shining. You are with friends. Good things are happening. Try not to focus too much on the past.'

I nodded numbly. She was right, of course. The only difficulty was, that the past made us who are now, and I knew I had to learn to accept this new version of me.

We walked along the River Seine. The crisp air cleared my head a little and I enjoyed hanging back and listening to the girls' chatter. We were stopped quite a few times by British servicemen still on patrol in Paris. They saw the British flag that Alice Kell was clutching and immediately came over to ask questions. Many of them wanted to have their photograph taken with Alice and other members of the team. And it wasn't only servicemen who stopped the girls – their presence in the city was obviously causing a stir and many locals requested autographs too.

'I feel like a famous person,' Flo giggled, flicking back her hair. 'Who would've thought that we would be well known in France?'

'Of course we're well known,' Alice joked back. 'We're the Dick, Kerr Girls – soon the whole of France will know about us!'

After our lengthy tour of the city, we returned to the hotel hungry and tired, and there was a huge collective sigh of relief once the food was served.

'Steak and chips!' Lily yelled, clattering her knife and fork. 'That's more like it!'

Before long, it was match night.

'We can't lose this game tonight,' Jessie said, as we

made our way back to the hotel to prepare after more sight-seeing. 'We need to start as we mean to go on.'

'Exactly. We have to believe we can win all our games,' Alice replied. 'And I'm confident that we can.'

'It seems odd playing on a Sunday, though,' Annie added. 'I was always taught that Sunday was the Sabbath.'

The others murmured their agreement. It certainly wasn't the done thing in England to play football on a Sunday. But the world was changing all the time. Maybe this was just another change we had to get used to.

We all walked to the Pershing Stadium together.

'Do you know,' I said to Hettie as we approached the main gates. 'I think I had my best sleep in a while last night.' This time, I was telling her the truth. My steps felt lighter, even with my limp, and my head was not as fuzzy and full of clutter.

'Perhaps it's the change in air?'

'Perhaps it is,' I replied.

It was quite clear once we were inside the stadium that a lot of people had come to watch the game. I heard whispers at the gate that there could be as many as twenty-two thousand.

Before the girls were whisked off by Mr Frankland

for a team talk, I managed to group them together for another team photograph. I wasn't going to miss any opportunity to capture the important moments with my camera.

The taller players, including Jessie, Lily and Alice Woods, stood up, their arms folded, their backs dead straight. At the front, the rest knelt on the ground, including Jennie, Flo and Alice Kell. As I took the shot, I noticed that some of the girl's smiles were quite nervous. Jennie was fiddling with her lip.

'Don't worry, girls. You can do it,' I called, as they began to move away.

'We know we can, Freddie!' Jessie called back, flashing me her familiar bright smile before she turned to join the others.

It was expected that the British Ambassador in Paris would be kicking off the match, but we heard before the game that he wouldn't be able to make it. The French Air Minister took his place, looking very important and grand.

Mr Frankland was acting as linesman and I noticed from my place on the sidelines that he was shooting concerned looks at the girls. I turned to Hettie.

'Is everything all right?' I asked her.

Hettie frowned a little. 'Mr Frankland is worried that the girls are nervous. This is a big game for them. He's worried they've put a lot of pressure on themselves.'

'I think they'll be fine.'

'I hope you're right, Freddie.'

The whistle blew and a shiver of anticipation ran through my body. I picked up my pen, ready to make notes. What would the people of Lancashire think of our girls now? Here, on French soil, ready to show another country what they were capable of. I would have to write up my notes quickly and arrange for a telegram to be sent to the newspaper so that they could run an early report.

The match began a little uncertainly, and it was clear that both sides were nervous. The Dick, Kerr Girls made sloppy passes, which was so unlike them, and for the first few minutes they all seemed to have difficulty maintaining their positions. The French team capitalised on this and made an early attack, sweeping down the left flank unmarked and driving the ball into the box. Luckily it sped past the goal. My stomach twisted a little.

Was this going to go badly?

However, this attack seemed to wake our girls up. They began to move the ball around more confidently and soon had the French team hemmed into their own half.

'This is better,' I whispered to Hettie.

We'd had no shots on target, but we were applying all the pressure. Surely it was only a question of time?

Sadly, I was mistaken. At the twenty-five-minute mark, a French winger, Mademoiselle Laloz, whizzed through the Dick, Kerr defence. She really was a remarkably quick player. She lifted the ball neatly and slotted it past Annie Hastie in goal.

1–0 to the French side.

The crowd cheered. Hettie and I groaned.

'It's all right,' I said, pointing. 'Look, Hettie. Our girls haven't given up. This has just put more fire in their bellies!'

The Dick, Kerr Girls took over possession and began to pile the pressure on. The poor French goalkeeper was under sudden bombardment, as shot after shot was driven towards her. It was only because she was such a remarkable keeper that the score didn't change.

'Come on!' yelled Hettie. 'Keep at it, girls. You're so close!'

'They have to score soon,' I said. 'It'd be unjust if they didn't.'

Thankfully, justice was served. Our girl, Minnie Lyons, picked up the ball from outside thirty yards and drove it so hard towards goal that the French goalkeeper, remarkable as she was, stood no chance.

1–1.

Hettie and I screamed in relief, along with the other English supporters in the crowd.

'Play up, Dick, Kerr's,' I heard them chant. 'Play up, Lancashire.'

As the whistle blew for half-time, I turned to Hettie, beaming.

'The French team are lucky to be drawing,' I told her. 'We're by far the better team here.'

The second half began quickly, and I was convinced that the Dick, Kerr Girls would score again. However, the French side seemed to be more industrious in their marking now and, in particular, our two strikers, Florrie Redford and Jennie Harris, found that they were unable to get the ball.

However, with only five minutes to go, everything changed. The French referee awarded what seemed like a fair corner to the Dick, Kerr Girls, but the

French team objected, claiming the ball had come off Florrie Redford's foot. The referee stood by his decision and the crowd roared with dissent.

'I don't like this,' I said to Hettie, pointing at a large section of the crowd that seemed to be moving towards the pitch. 'It could get ugly.'

I tugged on her arm, encouraging her to leave. As I did so, a wave of people began to run on to the pitch in protest, surrounding both teams. I saw the referee wildly blowing his whistle to call an end to the game, as local police began to swarm around the crowds. Luckily, our girls were able to calmly walk away with Mr Frankland, bemused expressions painted on all of their faces.

So, the first match was abandoned with five minutes to go. Who would've thought a women's game of football would end so dramatically? Mr Jackson would enjoy my match report, I was sure.

20

We left Paris for Roubaix the next morning. I woke early, feeling quite refreshed after a much better sleep. I had time to telegraph the first match report back to the office and then pen a short letter to Micky. I told him the result from yesterday and promised him that I would visit again on my return.

'It's good that you want to do that,' Hettie said, as she watched me carefully seal the letter. 'I think it will help both of you.'

The journey to Roubaix was a test in itself. I sat in the back of train, next to Hettie and opposite Mr Frankland. As we passed through the countryside, I couldn't help but stare at the damage that had been inflicted on the French towns of Chappelle, Briebiers, Houplines, Raimonte and Albert. It was much worse than the last train journey. Most houses and buildings were barely left standing. The sight chilled me down to the bone.

'It's awful,' Hettie said, peering out beside me.

I couldn't speak, so instead I numbly shook my head.

I thought of the number that must have perished here. The number of innocent souls that must have lost their homes and livelihoods. It made my head throb.

We passed deep trenches, still full of dark, dirty water. My throat constricted as I stared at the muddy graves. I remembered my feet trudging through similar mud in Belgium. I remembered the cold, the awful trenches, the cries of men around me. The gunfire.

My body trembled.

'Oh, Freddie.' Hettie gripped my sleeve.

I saw that she was looking at the twisted barbed wire entanglements that still surrounded the area. In places, I could just about see torn flecks of clothing trapped in it, and what I thought might be discarded shells littering the ground. I thought immediately of Johnnie, of his body, twisted on the ground. Dark thoughts swelled inside of me and I closed my eyes, willing them to go away.

'This should never happen again,' I whispered, my fingers gripping my leg. 'This can never happen again.'

Hettie stroked my arm carefully. 'You're right, Freddie. You are. But look! Recovery is happening. People are already rebuilding.'

I blinked and made myself look. Hettie was right.

I could see makeshift huts made from oil drums and wood. I saw people moving around the ruins, scavenging. Surviving. Starting over.

'They may be broken, but they're not beaten,' another voice said.

I looked up. I had completely forgotten Mr Frankland was there. He spoke quietly and didn't look at me. His gaze was also fixed on the homeless French villagers.

'People who haven't been to this part of France would never be able to conceive what these poor people have been through,' he said softly. 'They endured so much. They suffered greatly. But they will rebuild. They will rise again.'

I nodded. 'They will, you're right.'

'In life, you sometimes lose the battle,' Mr Frankland continued, his voice stronger now. 'But it's the greater war that's more important. We must always remember what it is we are fighting for.'

We arrived at the Roubaix stadium, perhaps with more anticipation than before. It was slightly smaller than the Paris venue, but we were told that over 16,000 spectators were there to see the girls play.

'That's a record for this ground,' the man at the gate

told us in broken English. 'It doubles the numbers we usually get.'

'Let's hope this lot don't flood the pitch if they don't like a decision,' Alice Kell quipped, and the rest of the team giggled. I noticed they were still shooting nervous looks at each other. No one was keen on another pitch invasion!

I took my usual position on the sidelines, notepad clutched in my hand, camera at the ready. Once again, Hettie sat next to me, telling me she liked the company.

When the French girls came out on to the pitch, they received a huge cheer from the crowd – a hero's welcome! I expected them to be more muted for our girls but to my surprise the crowd still roared, as if it was a cup final event. I saw many of the team smile in response as they waved to their chanting fans.

'Good old Dick, Kerr's!'

'Play up, Proud Preston!'

It made my chest swell with pride.

The first half was fast and furious, and the Dick, Kerr Girls once again kept the French team penned in their own half. Shots made by Lily and Jennie were saved by the nimble French keeper and other players such as Flo and Alice Kell put a couple of balls wide of goal.

I couldn't help but feel frustrated.

'We should be 5–0 here,' I muttered.

'I know,' Hettie said. 'But there's still a half to play – everything could change.'

Hettie was right. The second half started as the first had left off, at a blistering pace, and with the Dick, Kerr Girls taking control. Alice Woods made a move down midfield before making a well-timed and very accurate pass to Flo, who was just outside of the box. Flo barely hesitated and blasted the ball into the bottom left corner.

The crowd went wild.

1–0

'GOOD OLD DICK, KERR'S!'

'FLO REDFORD'S THE GIRL!'

'THAT'S HOW YOU DO IT!'

The pace didn't stop. Our girls continued to press and apply pressure. The French team, in response, looked beaten and worn out. Once again, it was only the amazing feats of their goalkeeper that kept the score at 1–0.

'We deserve more,' I muttered.

'Wait,' Hettie said calmly. 'There's ten minutes to go.'

And, as if my sister was a prophet, the game changed again. Alice Kell had managed to make a quick pass to

Jennie, who was in the penalty area. She looked sure to score until the French defender clattered in, late and panicking, and caught Jennie's shin with her boot, bringing her down.

'Penalty!' I shouted. Surely?

Fortunately, the referee agreed, blowing his whistle and pointing immediately to the spot. I glanced nervously at the crowd, wondering how they were going to react. But this time, they seemed to accept the decision and there was no pitch invasion.

Flo calmly placed the ball on the penalty spot.

'Come on, Flo,' Hettie muttered under her breath. 'You can do it.'

Flo calmly whipped the ball into the net with little hesitation.

2–0.

The crowd went wild. Union Jacks began to wave with abandon across the ground.

I made notes on my pad, my hand shaking with emotion. It felt so special to be here, to be part of this moment. I only wished that I could cap these feelings and carry them around with me for ever. I never wanted to forget it.

As the whistle blew, the crowd invaded the pitch

once again, but this time it was the British spectators, looking to congratulate their team. They picked up the girls and carried them around the pitch as if they were queens.

The queens of football.

The Dick, Kerr Girls had changed my life. They'd changed Hettie's too. They'd changed these spectators' lives – giving them joy and hope.

They'd changed everything.

We returned to the hotel bubbling with joy.

'I knew we could win it,' Alice Kell said, triumphantly. 'The French Ladies are so good at home and have improved so much since we last played them, but that just makes our win even more important.'

Jessie wrapped her arm around Alice. 'And we couldn't do it without you, Alice. You never stop believing in us. You are a true captain.'

As we approached the hotel, it was clear that there was a crowd gathered outside. A man strode forward.

'Ey up!' he said in a broad accent. 'Are you the Dick, Kerr Girls?'

Alice nodded shyly. 'Yeah, we are.'

The man's face immediately broke into a broad smile.

'You see, lads! I told you they'd be here!' He turned and gestured to the group of men gathered behind him. I could make out some soldiers, but there were others dressed in plain clothes.

'We all wanted to come and meet you,' the man explained. 'We're British soldiers, and men from Lancashire. We are part of the rebuilding programme, helping to get the French people back on their feet. We had to come and congratulate you. That was some game. You did our country proud.'

I could see that Alice's eyes were shimmering with tears. She was quite overcome.

Flo stepped forward. 'Thank you,' she said. 'That means a lot to us.'

'It's nowt.' He shrugged. 'We just needed you to know how happy it made us, seeing you play. You really are as good as any men I've seen on the pitch. You're our girls and we are proud to cheer you on.'

Mr Frankland stood beside me and breathed what sounded like a satisfied sigh.

'I have never seen a team get a better reception than ours have today,' he remarked.

'They seem to have that effect on people,' I replied.

Mr Frankland turned to me, his eyes sparkling.

'Oh, they do, Freddie. They really do.' He chuckled gently under his breath. 'I really think the whole world could end up falling in love with the Dick, Kerr Girls.'

'We are going to the Cenotaph this morning. Will you be all right with that?'

Hettie asked me this delicately as we left our rooms that morning. She hadn't been given much warning about the visit, but apparently Mr Frankland had decided it would be appropriate for the entire team to pay their respects and lay a wreath in memory of the many soldiers who had lost their lives.

'I'll be all right,' I assured her, squeezing her hand. 'Actually, I would like to do it too.'

As we walked down to the front of the hotel, I could see that Alice and Jessie were already struggling to lift the huge wreath that Mr Frankland had organised.

'How big is that thing?' I breathed.

'Oh, about twelve feet I think.' Hettie giggled. 'Bit of a heifer, eh?'

'I'd say!'

I felt bad watching the girls struggling with the arrangement as we made our way to the memorial.

I offered to help, but they would have none of it.

'You've got to think of your leg, Freddie,' Jessie scolded. 'We've already done so much walking this week.'

Hettie took my arm in hers. 'It's true, Fred. I've noticed you've been limping a bit. Especially after the climbing you did the other day. You need to be careful.'

'Oh, I'm quite all right,' I said casually, even though there was still a distinct ache there. I doubted it would ever really go. In honesty, I was more concerned with the other ache inside of me, the one that rested deep inside of my chest and only seemed to get stronger as we approached the cenotaph.

Could I really manage this?

The girls were getting quite emotional now, wiping their eyes and hugging each other. The war, of course, had sliced through all our lives in many different ways. Many of the team had lost loved ones.

As usual, my thoughts drifted to Johnnie. He had been a good man. He never deserved any of this.

Tears gathered in my eyes. I stifled back a choke and walked away from the group. I needed to be by myself.

Standing at a distance, I took deep lungs full of cool air and tried to steady my breathing. It was quiet here and, for one alarming second, it felt like Johnnie was standing next to me, his posture relaxed, a casual smile curling on his lips. It was silly really. I knew he wasn't there and yet . . . it was so easy to imagine.

I decided he would've liked it here. He would've liked the peace and quiet and the chance to pay his respects.

'I'm sorry,' I said quietly. 'We shouldn't have left you in that trench. Micky said you were gone. I know you probably were, but I still feel bad. Maybe you could've been saved. But I had to get out. I had to . . .'

The wind whipped around me, cold and piercing.

'I know you'd forgive me,' I whispered. 'You were like that, weren't you? You'd forgive me. You'd tell me to stop being a silly beggar and that I should get on with my life. But I just keep thinking – I keep thinking how I should've been stood where you were. You should never have been hit by that shell. I should have taken my place!'

Far away, I heard the sound of a crow cawing; its call sounded frantic and bleak. I shivered.

'I was meant to stand alongside you,' I said. 'We were brothers . . .' I paused. 'I know what you want me to do for Betsy. I know—'

There was a sound behind me, a gentle cough. I stiffened, my eyes blinking back warm tears.

'Freddie?'

I turned, startled. Jessie was standing behind me, dabbing her eyes with a hankie. She walked towards me; her face crumpled in concern.

'Freddie? Are you all right? I thought I heard you talking?'

I looked at the space where I imagined my friend standing. My brave, funny friend. A lad I was so fortunate to have known.

A light feeling drifted through me.

I breathed out. My body sagged a little, my head started to clear.

I looked up at Jessie. Her smile once again warmed me from the inside out. I blinked back my tears.

'Are you all right?' she asked again.

'I think so,' I replied. 'I think I'm starting to be.'

22

The crowd at Le Havre was the smallest of the tour. I guessed the number to be around 10,000, but the team didn't seem to mind. They were quick on to the pitch and eager to start.

I turned to Hettie. 'I have a good feeling about this game.'

'So do I.' She beamed back.

I hadn't ever seen the Dick, Kerr Girls play so fast and aggressively. They barely lost the ball and if they did, they were quick to win it back. By half-time, we were 3–0 up, thanks to two goals from Flo and a beautiful volley by Jennie.

Hettie was particularly impressed. 'I don't think they can lose this now.'

I had to agree with her. The second half started with the same speed and determination. The French team were barely able to touch the ball and at times seemed quite deflated. It wasn't long before Lily Lee passed a beautiful cross into the box, right at Flo's feet.

Flo didn't hesitate and curled it around the goalkeeper.

4–0 and a hat-trick for the glowing Florrie.

'She deserves that!' I said. 'She's played out of her skin today.'

Hettie nodded. 'They all have, to be fair. Every pass has been perfect.'

I watched as Jessie stormed through the midfield. She was so strong and quick footed. Looking up, she spotted Lily Parr free at the edge of the box. She passed quickly and Lily, on receiving it, turned neatly and powered the ball into the net. The goalkeeper stood no chance.

The crowd went wild, sounding far louder than 10,000-strong. Once again, I could hear the chants for the 'Lancaster Lasses'. I idly wondered how many French families would be going home tonight and talking about these amazing women from Preston.

'Lily Parr really does have quite a shot on her,' Hettie remarked. 'I think that could be the start of many goals to come.'

'I think you could be right there, Hettie.'

The game ended after another goal from the Dick, Kerr Girls, this time caused by a scrambled error in defence. The French team were not quick enough to clear the ball and Alice Wood was there to simply tap the ball in.

6–0.

'What a result!' I declared, watching as the girls ran around the pitch embracing one another. 'I actually think this team are getting better by the day.'

'Oh, they are,' Hettie replied, peering over at them in admiration. 'They really are. They could end up being the best team in the world.'

And who was I to argue?

After the thrilling final game, which we won 2–0 in front of a crowd of 14,000, there was a farewell party. The girls all looked wonderful dressed up in their fineries and I have to admit, even I scrubbed up well in my suit.

Hettie met me in the atrium and we walked into the hall together, arm in arm.

'You look very pretty,' I said, taking in her formal red dress. She was no longer my little sister. In fact, in many ways I felt like she was much older and wiser than me.

'Thank you,' Hettie replied shyly. 'You don't look too bad yourself.'

'We've done all right, haven't we?' I said, looking at the grand surroundings. 'Being a part of all this.'

'Sometimes I have to pinch myself and wonder what I've done to deserve it,' Hettie replied. 'But I can honestly say that working in that factory changed my life for the better. Meeting the girls, making friends and, yes, all of this . . .'

She gestured around the room. 'It's quite something, isn't it? I mean, these girls are just like us, Fred. They come from poor homes. They've had hard lives and yet now, they're in another country, being wined and dined. They've worked so hard for this. They followed their dreams.'

'I know.'

Hettie smiled warmly. 'I'm so glad you're part of this too, Freddie. I feel like it's helped you.'

I paused. My gaze drifted across the room, where I took in the sight of Mr Frankland laughing; of Alice Kell, Flo and Alice Woods talking animatedly to some of the French girls; of Lily Parr chatting shyly to the French manager. I felt a glowing feeling trickle through me. It was as comforting as supping warm milk. These girls were my family now, and I cared for each and every one of them.

'It has helped me in more ways than you know,' I said to Hettie.

Towards the end of the night, Jessie pulled me to one side. She squeezed my arm gently.

'I wanted to check in on you, Freddie. I wanted to make sure you were all right after yesterday?' She paused. 'It can't be easy being here so soon after the war.'

'I'm all right, Jessie.' I smiled weakly back at her.

'At the cenotaph . . .'

She hesitated; her gaze drifted to a spot behind me. 'At the cenotaph, I heard you talking to someone who wasn't there.'

I felt myself redden. 'It was nothing. I was a bit emotional. I . . .'

She squeezed my arm again. 'It's all right, Freddie. You don't need to sound so guilty. I know you were to talking to him.'

'To who?'

'To someone who died. It's obvious.' She sighed; a tiny shiver rippled through her body. 'I know that you've seen death, seen awful things. I know that you carry it about with you like a heavy suitcase.'

I nodded, slowly. 'Being there, at the cenotaph . . . it made me think about all of those things,' I admitted. 'But then—'

I stopped myself, sure of how silly I sounded.

Jessie peered up at me.

'Jessie . . . Do you believe in ghosts?'

I was glad she didn't laugh at me, but she took a moment or so before answering. Her expression was serious.

'I don't know,' she said, finally. 'I'd like to think there's something out there watching over us. And I do believe you find peace when you die.' She paused. 'Do *you* believe in ghosts?'

'I don't know. I'm not sure. But something happened to me.' I shook my head. 'It sounds so daft now, but I swear Johnnie was there somehow. I feel like he heard me.'

There was a brief silence.

'I'd like to think he did, too. And I'd also like to think that whatever happened to Johnnie, he would want you to stop hurting. He's not the only one.'

I nodded weakly. 'I'll try,' I said.

I'll really try.

Because maybe it was time to live the way my friend would want me to.

It was time to do right by Johnnie.

We are trudging through the ruins of the Belgian villages. Johnnie is limping and his arm is hidden under his jacket. I know that his injuries run deeper under there, but I don't want to see them.

'You're back,' I say.

'To be honest, I never really left.'

'What's it like?'

'What? Being dead?' He shrugs. 'It's not so bad. It's not how you imagine it to be.'

We stop walking and take in the scene around us – the broken buildings, the splintered wood, the deep, swamp-like trenches.

'It's all so pointless, isn't it? War,' he says. 'All of this, and for what?'

'I don't know.'

'Things need to change, Fred. Lads like you need to be part of the change.'

'What do you mean?'

'There will be more wars. But you need to be there, picking

up the pieces, rebuilding. Don't let them forget what war does.'

'Surely no one will forget that?'

He smiles at me. 'I expect they will. People do, don't they? Help them remember what is most important.'

I frown. 'But do I really know what is important?'

He looks at me and that cheeky grin that I remember so well is back. I don't think I will ever forget it.

'Of course you know, Freddie, because you've been lucky enough to have it all your life.'

'But...'

'Just look around you,' he says faintly. 'Just look around you and you'll see it.'

I wake with three words floating in my mind. Love. Community. Friendship.

The journey home is a long one. We are all tired and, as a group, quite content to be quiet in our thoughts. I can't help thinking what Johnnie would have made of this team. I know for a fact he would have been impressed by their skills, but I think he would have been excited by their potential too. Johnnie believed in sport. He knew that it brought people together. He would have valued that above everything else.

'The French team want to arrange more games in the future,' Mr Frankland told me and Hettie on the ferry back to Dover. 'They are keen for this to be the start of an ongoing relationship.'

'And so it will,' Hettie said warmly. 'The Dick, Kerr Girls bridge the gaps between countries.'

'They certainly do that,' Mr Frankland agreed. He gazed at the players, who were huddled together in conversation; they really were quite the team – not a girl looked out of place, each one was fully included.

'I always suspected this team was capable of amazing things,' he said. 'But they continue to surprise me.'

As if on cue, one of the girls broke out in a hearty laugh that set the rest of the girls off.

'Here's to the rest of the season,' I said, raising an imaginary glass. 'May it continue in the same way – with strength, success and lots and lots of laughter.'

Mr Frankland chuckled slightly as that idea took hold. 'Yes, you are right. Let's wish for that. To well-deserved laughter and friendship. For without that, we wouldn't be here, would we?'

I thought of Johnnie once again.

'It's true. Friendship means everything.'

***

By the time we arrived back at Spa Road, I was feeling exhausted and I knew Hettie felt the same. We were both quiet as we walked down the cobbled street and only began to talk again when we saw our little terrace house come into view.

'I can't believe we're home again so soon,' Hettie said, pausing just outside the front door. 'These past days have just flown by.'

'They really have.'

She shook her head in disbelief. 'Honestly, Freddie, my life has changed so much.'

'The war changed me,' I said suddenly. 'It really did. I'll never be the same lad that I was when I left home that day. I was so innocent back then, I had so little direction, I was so naive ...'

'Oh, Freddie!'

'No, no. It's all right, our kid.' I turned to her and grinned. 'I think I'm getting used to the person that I am now. I know that I have a limp. I know that my head hurts and feels muddled at times. I know my footballing days are over and my sleep may always be disturbed, but ...' I hesitated, trying to find the right words. 'I'm happy now. I'm doing something I love. I'm with people I respect and I really do think things will get better.'

'They will!'

We looked at each other and a warm, familiar feeling surged through me. I remembered all the times I had spent with Hettie, mucking around with her, teaching her to play football, taking her to school.

'You're a good sister,' I said. 'I'm so proud of you.'

Her eyes watered. She blinked and then sniffed. 'Oh, Freddie, you daft apeth. I'm proud of you too. I always will be.' She reached for my hand and took it in hers. 'Are you ready to go inside now? Mam will be frantic . . .'

I nodded. I was ready.

I was glad to be home.

Inside was warm, like a toasty stove. I could smell bread in the oven and my stomach growled.

Mam was first to greet us, sweeping us up into a huge hug.

'Oh, I've missed you both so much, you can't imagine. Were they good to you out there? Did they look after you? Have you been eating properly? Washing?'

Her barrage of questions was quite overwhelming, but we answered each one as best we could.

Dad was standing further back . He waited until Mam had stopped her questions and then approached me slowly.

'All right, Dad?'

'All right, son?'

He slapped my back and coughed loudly.

'How was it?'

I nodded. 'It was good. Really good, in fact. I think the newspaper will be pleased with the pictures I took.'

His nod was slow and deliberate. 'Aye, I saw the editor from your newspaper, as it goes. He was drinking down at the pub.'

'Really?'

'Really.' Dad rubbed his chin. 'Singing your praises, he was, saying you will make a fine reporter.'

I stepped back, feeling a little shocked. 'He said that?'

'Yes, he did.' He smiled. 'I'm pleased for you, son. You're doing so well.'

'Are you?' I stammered, still feeling a little stunned. 'Are you really pleased?'

'Aye. Don't doubt yourself again, son. You're a good lad. A smart one. You're going to be quite all right.'

I held his gaze; my speech now felt steady.

'Yes, Dad, I will be,' I said quietly. 'I really will be.'

Alone upstairs, I placed my suitcase under my bed and sat for a moment or two in the silence. Then, after a long, drawn-out breath, I reached inside my drawer.

The photograph was right at the back, still a little crumpled, but in remarkably good shape considering its journey.

I stared at it for a bit, taking in her sad, serious eyes, her half-smile and dark, glossy curls.

She was a pretty lass.

'Hello, Betsy,' I said. 'I'm coming to find you, like I promised. I'm going to tell you all about Johnnie's war. I'll tell you how wonderful he was and how brave he was at the end.'

I hesitated, a sob choking in my throat.

'And I will tell you that he was the best friend I could ever have.' I paused, my voice barely a whisper now. 'He was much more than that. He was my brother.'

Later, Hettie and I sat on the front doorstep, watching as Martha played football with the boys from the street.

She was running at full pelt across the cobbles, the ball was at her feet and a red-faced Ronnie was at her tail. She quickly took the ball on her left foot and eased it into the makeshift goal.

Her arms began to pump the air, her face was alight with joy.

'Goal!' she screamed.

Then, seeing that we were watching her, she ran towards us, her hair whipping back in the wind.

'Did you see that, Hettie? Freddie? Did you see what I just did? I scored a cracker!'

'She's all right – for a girl,' Ronnie muttered. He collected the ball from behind the wall of coats and glared at Martha. 'She was lucky, though.'

'I did it! I beat a boy! Again!' Martha said, grinning. 'I've proved I'm just as good as them now.'

I smiled back at her and ruffled the top of her sweaty head.

'Yes, you are, lassie,' I whispered. 'You really are.'

Martha and the Dick, Kerr Girls were the part of our new future.

And how very bright that future was!

HAVE YOU READ THE FIRST
BOOK IN THE SERIES?

LACE UP YOUR BOOTS AND GET READY FOR KICK OFF — THE NEXT DICK, KERR GIRLS NOVEL IS COMING SOON . . . !

ABOUT THE AUTHOR

Eve Ainsworth is an award-winning author, creative workshop coordinator and public speaker, who draws from her extensive work with teenagers to write authentic, honest and real novels for young people.

Eve is also a passionate football fan and although being born with two left feet, she can often be found on a cold Saturday afternoon cheering on her son from the sidelines.

Eve lives in Crawley, West Sussex with her husband, two young children and slightly crazy dog.

IF YOU LIKE THIS, YOU'LL LOVE . . .

What if you could conjure the clouds?

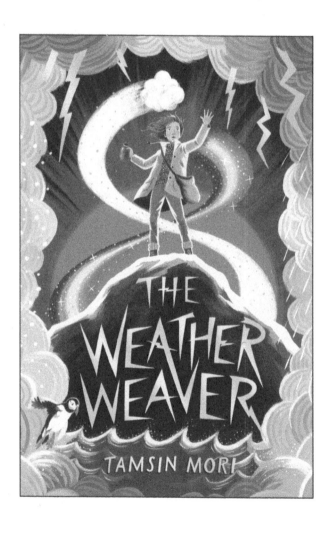

Dare you travel to Inchtinn – where sinister beings stir and tormented souls seek revenge? What if survival relies on facing your greatest fears?

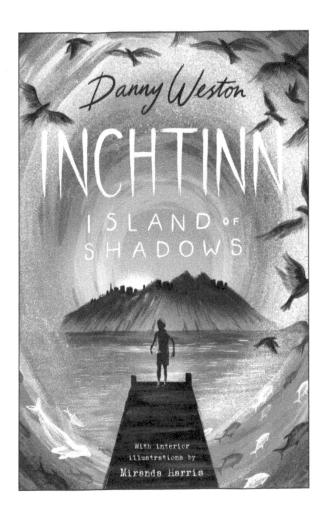

The first book in a gripping new fantasy
adventure series from New York Times
bestselling author, A. J. Hartley.

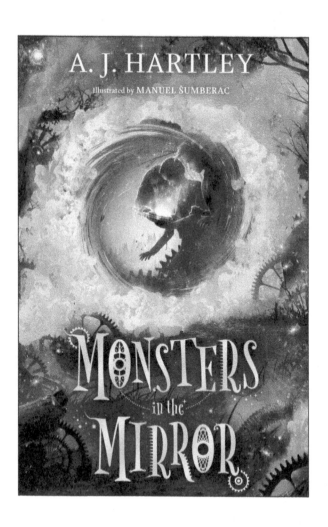

A. J. HARTLEY

Illustrated by MANUEL ŠUMBERAC

MONSTERS
in the
MIRROR

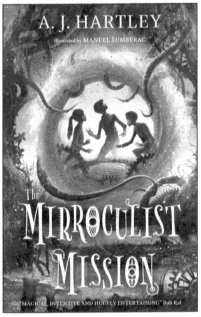

'A wonderfully written, delightful story, full of diverse characters, from a hugely talented author. Highly welcome and recommended'
Bali Rai

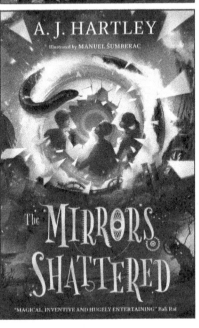

'Brilliant, brilliant, brilliant. A. J. Hartley is a true master of the written word'
Christopher Eccleston

The first book in a new electrifying series
from author of *Sky Thieves*, Dan Walker.

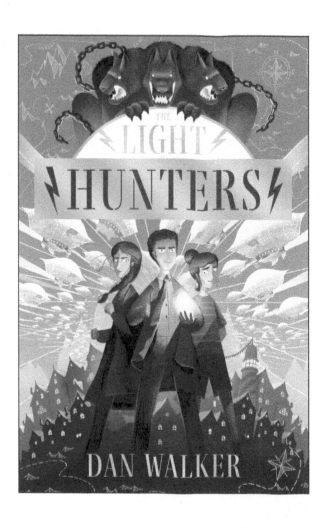

A rollicking medieval romp where laughter
and action abound in equal measure . . .
And where danger lurks around every corner.

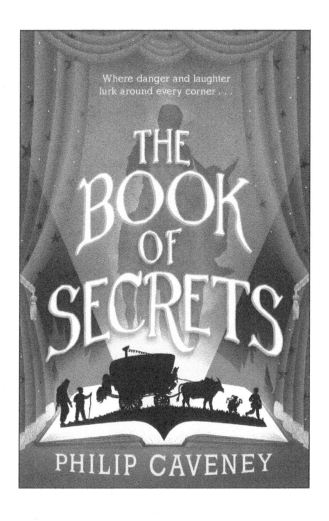

Where danger and laughter
lurk around every corner . . .

THE
BOOK
OF
SECRETS

PHILIP CAVENEY

HAVE YOU EVER WONDERED
HOW BOOKS ARE MADE?

UCLan Publishing are based in the North of England and involve BA Publishing and MA Publishing students from the University of Central Lancashire at every stage of the publishing process.

BA Publishing and MA Publishing students are based within our company and work on producing books as part of their course – some of which are selected to be published and printed by UCLan Publishing. Students also gain first-hand experience of negotiating with buyers, conceiving and running innovative high-level events to leverage sales, as well as running content creation business enterprises.

Our approach to business and teaching has been recognised academically and within the publishing industry. We have been awarded Best Newcomer at the Independent Publishing Guild Awards (2019) and a *Times* Higher Education Award for Excellence and Innovation in the Arts(2018).

As our business continues to grow, so too does the experience our students have upon entering UCLan Publishing.

To find out more, please visit
www.uclanpublishing.com/courses/